Unrest

EMMA CÔTÉ

WINNER OF THE 43RD ANNUAL 3-DAY NOVEL CONTEST

ANVIL PRESS

Library and Archives Canada Cataloguing in Publication

Title: Unrest / Emma Côté.
Names: Côté, Emma, author.
Identifiers: Canadiana 20220158045 | ISBN 9781772141900 (softcover)
Classification: LCC PS8605.O87355 U57 2022 | DDC C813/.6—dc23

Cover image: Reilly Ballantyne
Book design: Derek von Essen

Represented in Canada by Publishers Group Canada
Distributed by Raincoast Books

The publisher gratefully acknowledges the financial assistance of the Canada
Council for the Arts, the Canada Book Fund, and the Province of British
Columbia through the B.C. Arts Council and the Book Publishing Tax Credit.

Anvil Press Publishers Inc.
P.O. Box 3008, Station Terminal
Vancouver, BC V6B 3X5 Canada
www.anvilpress.com

PRINTED AND BOUND IN CANADA

To my desk angel, Zoé Duhaime, who helped
me stay afloat and on course more than once.

"Death will be a great relief. No more interviews."
— Katharine Hepburn

Prologue

THIS IS MY favourite part. I know that sounds strange to say, because Mr. Redgers is dying and all, but I don't think I'll ever get sick of being here for the final moments like this. It doesn't feel sad anymore. Not the way seeing the people left behind used to feel. Or the way I used to make myself feel afterwards so that I could block it all out.

"I'm going to touch your feet now, Mr. Redgers, is that okay?"

He doesn't really respond, he makes kind of an "Uh," sound like he's agreeing with me, but I know he means yes. I've been learning to speak his language for weeks now, so that I can provide him the best care.

The snow is falling outside his cabin window, so I make sure to tell him what it looks like. I tell him about the size of the snowflakes, how long they are taking to fall to the ground. He loves the perfect view of the snow-peaked mountains in the background, so I try to describe the waning light for him, how it makes the facets look like they're shifting, alive. He can't see his favourite view anymore, because his eyes are closed now. It won't be long.

I press my thumbs into the soles of his feet and slide them up toward his toes. Then back down again, and up. Up and down. I see the corners of his mouth flicker, ever so slightly, in delight. The feet are what always go cold first, as his are right now. It's funny how there's such a standard process to something that totally *mystifies* people. Shocks most people into disbelief, even though there's a universal guarantee that it's coming for us all.

Before he arrived, we discussed what other things he would want by his bedside, and I made sure I had them all ready for him. Vanilla scented candles are placed around the room, but not so many to make the smell overpowering, just a whiff when I move, shifting the air. An old record player crackles from the back corner, Satie's *Gymnopédie No.1* drifts around us like a cloud.

Mr. Redgers also requested orchids, which were hard to get at this time of year, this high up in the mountains, in the middle of nowhere. But Mr. Redgers is an ideal client. He found me over a year ago, and we started planning together. So I had time to source the exact colour, and shape, and number of orchids he wanted. A western prairie fringed orchid, a Hochstetter's butterfly orchid, and finally, a ghost orchid, because Mr. Redgers can't resist a good joke. The orchids will all live on for five or six months after he's gone, but we have a plan for that too.

"You can let go now, Mr. Redgers. I'm here. You're safe."

It isn't like it is in the movies, it's slower and sweeter. His chest deflates slowly and his mouth goes slack. I move up toward him to brush his hair a final time.

"Time of death, 8:53 p.m., December 21, 2015."

Chapter One

I HATE STORIES that start off like the one I'm about to tell you, but I don't think there's any other way to tell this one without losing your attention completely. The thing is, if I just start at the beginning, you'll likely find it much too bleak to go on. So for the sake of your soul, this story has a happy ending, it just takes a while to get there.

I manage just fine without a mother. That's what I tell myself anyway. I manage just fine without a father too, but he's been gone so long I can barely remember what it was like to have one in the first place. Though I wasn't an orphan or anything, not exactly. So don't feel bad for me, honestly. I can feel you wanting to get sentimental about it, but I've found a way to use my own experiences to help others. People love that detail. It gives them strength. I slip in the detail about my father's death at the most opportune moment when I'm at work, and my clients grab on to it like a life raft. Plus, I did have a mom for a lot of my life. Well in theory anyway. We haven't spoken in fifteen years. Though now that she's gone too, I guess not much has changed.

It was a chilly spring day in Cleveland, the type of day that made you feel like maybe the world is going to forget about summer that year. Like it would stay frigid and barren for another six months.

I've never liked winter, and the seemingly endless ones in Cleveland often make me wonder why I chose it as my home. Because a choice is exactly what it was. As is everything.

The phone call came in the early afternoon. I remember that it struck me as odd because I came home a bit early from work. I had a cold that day, and I'm not any good to a grieving family if I'm sitting there sniffling and blowing my nose as well. Oh, I'm a funeral director. Did I mention that already? I don't think I did. I own my own funeral home and everything, but we'll get to that later. I had been working long hours lately and I was already feeling a weariness creeping into my bones that felt way beyond my thirty-three years.

The even weirder thing was that I *knew* something was wrong when I walked into my house that day. Unfortunately, some things just stick with you. The feeling was the exact same as the one I felt back in high school, right before everything changed. Big events have a way of shifting the energy in the room before mere humans have any idea that our entire existence is about to tilt.

Okay, so maybe I need to go back even further. This happens all the time when I'm trying to tell a story. I pick a starting point and then remember, there's still more you need to know. So we rewind to when I was eleven years old and I had just got back from school, a highly scored test safely tucked away in my backpack. After I walked into the house, I noticed it was strange that my mother wasn't there to greet me. Somehow, she always made it home to do that. I crept through the house pretending I was an intruder.

"Mom?" I yelled when the game wasn't fun anymore.

I heard my mother clear her throat. When she responded, her voice was tight and distant and sounded as if she was expecting a different person entirely. "Mylène? Is that you? What time is it?"

I found her in the bedroom, crumpled Kleenex covered nearly the entire bed like a floating blanket.

"What's going on?" I asked, unable to tear my eyes away from the tissues.

"It's about your father."

I had never been particularly close to my father, but I was fond of his presence. If nothing else, I appreciated that he was there, in my life, a constant.

"What happened?" I said.

"There was an accident." My mother, Cerise, looked away then, and I stared down at my shoes. I remember that one of my laces was untied. My heart was pounding noisily against my chest, and I thought briefly of telling it to shut up. "A car accident," my mother continued, as if I was a baby and couldn't put two and two together. But even then, I realized it was just one of those things, one of those things you have to say in order for it to be true.

I looked around the room then, as if I was searching the corners for something that might hint at the fact that my mother had this all wrong. I saw my father's tie, the one he had been wearing the day before, draped over the edge of the chair he always sat on to take off his shoes.

"Is he…" I couldn't bring myself to say the word.

My mother looked up at me finally, her eyes were bloodshot, like she'd been swimming in a vat of chlorine. I think she knew she was supposed to stay strong for me, but I'm not sure if she tried.

"I'm so sorry," Cerise said.

Okay, that was pretty bad, I'll admit. And the truth is that it gets worse before it gets better. But stick with me here.

So years later, when I was eighteen and deciding what I wanted to do for the rest of my life, I thought it would be just weird and gross and morbid enough if I went to mortuary school.

"Oh, that poor Andrews girl is so sad and obsessed with death. Of course she would take on something so *ominous*. Poor thing.

And have you seen her mother lately? Lord help her."

I could hear them whisper these types of things behind my back, and that made me want to do it all that much more. In the State of Ohio, you can become a funeral director in about two years — half the length of time it takes to get an actual degree, and twice as useful. Death and taxes, right? Oddly enough, the State also requires that you complete one year at an accredited university *before* your year at mortuary school. So I took classes on psychology and business so that I would be prepared to open my own company as soon as possible. I got really good at making plans when I was young, because nobody else was stepping up to the job.

My mother sort of fell off the face of the planet after my father died. But more on that later. I don't want you getting confused.

So I graduated from mortuary school with a plan: a couple years as an apprentice and then open my own funeral home. Funeral directors can make some serious bank after just a couple of years you know, so it's worth it. Okay, I know what you're thinking, you're wondering if I feel bad playing into the sometimes extortionate system we have in place to further torment the grieving? And I see where you're coming from. The average cost of a funeral in Ohio can be anywhere between $2,700 and $10,000, plus interest if the poor, grieving widow can't pay the cost upfront and the dead, dumb husband didn't bother to get himself any life insurance. Who am I to change a system that's clearly working for me?

Like pretty much everything else except motherhood, the funeral industry used to be dominated by men. But in recent years, nearly 60% of mortuary science students have been women. I don't know why there's been such a sudden shift. Maybe all of their parents died too, but what I do know is that it's a smart move to make. Because the industry brings in sixteen *billion* dollars a year just in the USA alone. Can you believe that? I mean it probably makes sense now that you know a thing or two about the numbers. And thankfully, death isn't something that scares me anymore, not my own anyway, but you could definitely say I have a sixth sense about it. I can feel it coming, like a shift in the barometric pressure, warning of a storm.

So that's how I knew something was up that day when I came home from work early, but it had been so many years since I'd felt that sense of offness that I didn't recognize it right away. I walked around my one-bedroom apartment, touching my items, making sure nothing was out of place. Perhaps I had been robbed instead? I straightened the yellow throw pillows on my couch, which was re-upholstered in a vintage teal velvet. When I got to my desk, my fingers reflexively reached above it, to the one piece of art I owned; a small oil painting of a bowl of fruit, with a human skull sitting where an apple should be. I tilted my head from side to side as I looked at the painting, as if it might shift or change. When I was certain the image wasn't going to mutate, I took a scan of my own body. I ran my fingers over my flaming red hair, pinned up in 1940s victory rolls, and inspected the seams of my vintage, zebra print blouse. Everything was still in its rightful place; my retro appearance and my subsequent rejection of how a funeral director should be.

It wasn't until I was back in the kitchen, boiling water for a cup of tea, that I noticed the little red light flashing on my answering machine. And before you say it, yes, I have heard of voicemail. I have it at the funeral home, of course, amidst the calming shades of beige and soft fabrics. But in my own home I prefer all things retro, as you well know, and let's face it, answering machines have arrived.

"Nobody ever calls me at home," I said aloud. "Let alone leaves a message."

The fear was instant, as it seemed to me that it could only be bad news. Nobody would bother leaving a message for anything else.

You'd have to have friends, or a partner, or a life for that. I pressed play and held my breath.

"Hello, this is Randal Lahola, executor of Cerise Andrews' estate. I'm very sorry to do this via message, but I'm calling to inform you of your mother's passing. There are a few things here that need to be sorted out before we can move forward with anything else. Please call me back at this number at your earliest convenience. Again, I'm very sorry for your loss."

I tilted my head to the side, as if I'd forgotten altogether that I had a mother and that she could, in fact, die.

Chapter Two

So we're officially caught up now. There's more stuff that would do you well to know. But we'll get to it later, because it's just a *lot* to take in all at once.

"Mylène, I'm so sorry," Katie says when I drop my books off at the library the following day. Katie is a solid woman, with deep-set crow's feet, and a presence that welcomes you in. I told her that my mother had died when she asked how I was today, because I'm so used to dealing with death that it didn't even occur to me to lie. Well not lie, exactly, but soften the truth. Katie and I aren't close the way friends are close, but we've been in a book club together for years.

"Thank you, but you know, her and I weren't that close," I say.

"I know you've never really mentioned her before, but still... she was your Mom, right. That's got to be complicated."

"Grief is always complicated," I say. "That's true." It's a line that I often feed to my clients when they break down in tears, the slobbering uncontrollable kind, the kind that makes the women feel like they need to start apologizing. The first thing I do is hand them a tissue, place a hand on their shoulder, and look them in the eyes while saying, "Grief is always complicated. Don't apologize for feeling any of it."

Katie looks around the library, toward the non-fiction section.

I can see that she's about to recommend a book to help with the grief, but then thinks twice.

"So do you have to head upstate? To sort out her affairs?"

"Yeah, I do actually."

"What will you do about your business? Obviously people aren't going to stop dying."

The colour drains slightly from Katie's face when she says this. She isn't sure if she's offended me, if her joke was in bad taste or not. I obviously haven't allowed her to get to know me that well. I smile. "No, it's a bit of a planetary epidemic, isn't it?"

Katie sighs, relieved. Maybe she would be worth getting to know on a deeper level after all. I'm about to ask her if she wants to go out for a coffee. It might be nice to talk to somebody about death, instead of comforting others for a change. But the phone rings and Katie gives me a little, sad smile and side steps to the receiver.

• • •

I haven't been back to my hometown in fifteen years, and it feels both devastating and reassuring to see that nothing has changed. The single road leading in and out of town is still lined with modest homes, and as I roll in at nearly ten o'clock on a Friday evening, I am struck by how barren the streets are. A solitary set of headlights swings by up ahead, and I feel confident that whomever is behind the wheel is going to carefully drive the speed limit the rest of the way home and then go directly to bed.

It takes half a day of driving to get there from Cleveland, so among other reasons, Cerise stopped asking for me to visit long ago. Besides, I think that she has been happy to live her little life, in her little town with her little friends. And yes, I call my mother by her first name, by the way. It just seemed like a more realistic thing to do.

Standing in front of my childhood home, I exhale a long breath, unwilling to let in any of the pesky emotions that are gnawing at my ankles. Randal Lahola explained that the house was almost entirely sorted except for one closet in Cerise's bedroom, which is still full of her things. It had been clearly stated in the will that I was to be contacted to make the final arrangements and clean it out.

The numbness coursing through my veins worries me slightly. Isn't a person who has lost their only remaining relative meant to feel a bit more…distraught? But it seems the hysterical version of myself died years ago.

Walking in the front door of the home, the first thing I notice is the smell. Like mouldy potatoes and burnt dust. I slowly make my way toward the back of the house, to my mother's bedroom, feeling like an intruder. The walls are still the same beige they've always been, and the linoleum floors are scuffed and worn in all the same places, including where I once put on a pair of ancient roller skates and went up and down the hallway four times before Cerise blew in, screaming for me to stop.

My mother's bedroom still sports the same quilt, sewn together from old baby clothes that I'd outgrown. I sit down on the bed, the same one my mother had been curled up in the day I learned that my father was dead.

"God, this is fucking depressing," I say to the beige. "Let's get this over with." But even as I say it, I wonder what it is that I want to get back to, or if I'm just looking to be anywhere but here. My life in Cleveland has been feeling exceptionally dull lately. It wears on you eventually, the funeral industry. But what else is a bored funeral director to do with such a specified skillset?

Regardless, it is almost impossible to be sad about the death of a woman I no longer knew. My mother held that title in name only by the time she died. Although at first, I did hold on hope that one day we would find our way back to each other. After the first five years without contact, I eventually gave up. And then I managed to stop thinking about her altogether. So thankfully, it just feels like a ghost has stopped haunting me.

It doesn't take long for me to organize my mother's affairs, because it isn't a sentimental process. Again, don't feel bad. It's totally fine. Rain is falling softly outside the bedroom window, urging me to finish the job before the roads become un-drivable. My pile of things to throw away takes up nearly the entire floor. The only thing that seems worth keeping is the quilt, and I have to admit that if that was all I got from this godforsaken journey, it would likely be enough.

That's when I find them, stuffed in the back of a closet under a long-forgotten pair of skinny jeans. A small stack of something, wrapped in brown packaging paper, without an address. I untie the piece of twine holding the whole thing together.

It's a small postcard, accompanied by about half a dozen others. Instinctively, I flip the first one over, and I'm shocked to find it addressed to me.

Chapter Three

ON ONE SIDE it has a picture of the skyline in Cleveland, and my heart beats a little faster as I take it in. It looks kind of familiar and weirdly foreign at the same time. I've lived in Cleveland since college, but I never really saw the city as a tourist destination. Seeing the photograph attached to a postcard makes me wonder what I've been missing about the city.

Lakeview Cemetery
Cleveland, Ohio
March 23, 2011
Dear Mylène,

You know, I still love your name. It's always sounded like the start of a song to me. Sometimes, when I was working at the factory, I would just repeat your name over and over in my head with every item that passed on the line. It made me feel connected to you. I bet that surprises you. It's so much easier to say these things in writing.

Anyway, I'm here in Cleveland. I came to visit you, but I couldn't bring myself to pick up the phone, or just show up after all these years. So instead I started wandering around until I eventually found myself at the Lakeview Cemetery. Who knew such a breathtaking chapel was hiding in a graveyard? I sat in awe, staring up at the stone columns and ornate stained glass for what felt like hours. And then I wandered in between the tombstones, or I think they're called headstones, right? And all through the grounds. And I have to admit, I felt peaceful. I think it's the closest I've felt to you in nearly twenty years. You loved going to cemeteries even when you were a little girl. I never understood it, but I'm trying to now..

Yours,

Cerise

I reread the postcard twice to ensure I'm not hallucinating the whole thing. But both times it makes my lip curl in disgust. I hate that I have a French name and no ability to speak the language. I hate even more that my mom does too. It's not even her real name, Cerise. Well, obviously not because that's a fruit. It was a nickname my father gave her, and she refused to be called anything else. It made me shudder when she would introduce herself as such. But then again, I could find fault in the way she blinked.

I spread the postcards out on the bed, looking from one photograph to the next. They are all fairly unfamiliar places to me, considering I've barely left my home state. I wonder how my mother chose them all. Then I flip all the postcards over so that the words are showing and sure enough, they are all addressed to me.

Without another thought I gather up the postcards, stuff them along with my guilt into a bag, and tear out of the room, dialing the executor's number on my way.

"I'm done at the house," I say. "List it, sell it, I don't care. Just keep me as far out of it as you can."

Chapter Four

BACK IN CLEVELAND, the wind is still racing off the lake and through the streets. Looking at the urn filled with my mother's ashes, I feel empty. There had been no funeral planned. She requested that she be cremated and delivered back to the house for me to do with her, "What I saw fit." What an honour. So now I'm stuck with her. Dealing with death every day, you start to think of it as more of a transactional interaction than a life altering thing. And death doesn't look the same on each person. Some families come in, having already moved through denial and found acceptance in a matter of days. Those are the lucky ones. I always assume that they probably had good relationships with the deceased. That they called every Sunday and told them what they had for dinner. That was never going to be me anyway, so now my mother's death is more like putting a period at the end of a sentence.

When I was a kid, I'd always felt a bit secretive about my life. I figured most kids were. Once you know how to wipe your own butt and bathe yourself with minimal trauma, well your parents' usefulness sometimes starts to shift. You want to exert your independence, right? But at some point, usually, you start to drift back. You start to realize you don't know everything and that maybe you do need your parents. But right around the time that would have been slated to happen was when my dad died, and my mom basically died along with him.

I tried for years to get her to come back to herself, to come back to me. But it never seemed like we got anywhere. She stayed on bereavement leave until her boss at the factory had to let her go. He did it with as much compassion as he could. And from then on it was like my mother filled each room with fog as she passed through it.

By the time I was eighteen, I'd had enough. I worked two part-time jobs, and made sure to hold onto my straight As in school. There was no way I was going to support her anymore, and there was no way she was going to pay for my college. So I did what I had to do. I'm sure some people thought that I was harsh, leaving her there without a plan. But it isn't a daughter's job to take care of a mother, alright? Do you hear me? Sorry, I just get a little worked up about that sometimes. Even though I don't think anybody would ever fault me for what I did.

It was late summer, right before I was set to go away to school. I picked U of C because it was moderately respected and it had ivy-covered buildings in the summertime. What can I say? I had very little guidance. When I got accepted I went into my mother's bedroom — her permanent hideaway by that point — to tell her I got in. It smelled stale, like stiff, unwashed socks.

"Cerise, I got into U of C," I said. "Can you believe it?"

"That's great, Mylène. I'm happy for you. Are you going?"

"What kind of question is that? Of course I'm going. What else would you expect me to do?" Cerise just shrugged and turned over, and that was as much as I could take. A week later, I filled all the cupboards and stuffed the fridge with produce. I put $1,000 in an envelope on the kitchen counter and left without saying goodbye.

So it's not like I'm expecting anything to be different when I get back to Cleveland. If anything, this is a relief. And I know what you're thinking, this is horrible! Quel désastre! Poor Mylène, with the cute French name, even though she doesn't speak French. What a horrible, sad, empty little life. But it isn't really that way. Like I told you, you don't have to feel bad for me. I'm not an orphan, I'm just free of family. I'm free to be whomever I want.

Chapter Five

I'VE HEARD THAT if you tell somebody to think of their happy place, the vast majority of people will picture somewhere in nature. A peaceful meadow, listing in the breeze, or a tropical beach, untouched by tourists.

For me, my happy place is my preparation room. You wouldn't think that embalming bodies would be so soothing. There are parts of it that are borderline sociopathic, like poking needles into a person's lungs to drain them of gas, for example. But mortuary science is described as an art *and* a science for a reason. We get to style a person for their very last party. And that's quite an honour. I love all the liquids and levers, the wooshing and pumping of the machines, and the methodical development of the whole process. I'll spare you the dirty details, obviously, I'm not delusional enough to think that everybody wants to know how a mortician goes about the whole thing. But nowhere do I feel as serene and focused as I do in this room.

Today I'm working on a little old lady that died peacefully in her sleep, at the end of a long life. The perfect end to an un-perfect story, or so I assume, since nothing is ever perfect. I love taking care of the little old ladies the best. The funerals just aren't that sad. They've lived, people get it, they accept. You live, you grow old, you die, that's pretty much the goal. Plus their hair is really soft.

Her name is Miss Geller. She was ninety-eight years old, and she was in good health until the day she died. Miss Gellar never owned a car, opting instead to walk around town or take the bus. So maybe that's the secret. She also never bothered getting married, so maybe the secret is something else entirely. She lived alone until she was ninety-five, and then her family decided they didn't have the time to care for her anymore and put her in a home. An Active Senior Living Centre. She could only take it for three years and then she basically said, "Well if this is all there is, I guess I'll head out." It would be awful, wouldn't it? Being stuck in one of those homes? Ohio is still miles behind when it comes to medical assistance in dying. But it takes a long time for things to change. I digress.

"How are you doing today, Miss Gellar?" I say as I take my make-up and brushes out of the drawer. You have to use a different type of make-up for the deceased, because their skin isn't warm and malleable in the same way as the living. When I'm done, I take a step back and admire my handiwork. Miss Gellar looks as if she's sleeping peacefully, dreaming about all the ways she's managed to win the lottery of life.

The phone rings in the office and I cross Miss Gellar's hands and place them on her stomach. Then I step back and remove my gloves and mask.

I chose the name Gateway Funeral Home for my business, because I thought it had a nice feel to it. I'm not a religious woman. When I was a kid, I never pictured my father sitting in a white robe, raising a glass with Honest Abe or anything. But I'm not a soulless under-taker either, people tend to get that all wrong. I went to mortuary school because I was already familiar with death, and I thought it would make for a stable career. I was forced to become pragmatic as a teenager, but becoming a lawyer, doctor, or psychologist all seemed like too much school and money and time. And while I don't necessarily think of death as a gateway into the afterlife, I think it can most certainly be a gateway into whatever stage is next for those left behind.

So as you can see I don't have a ton of people to talk to other than grieving families and corpses. That's why I'm telling you all of this. It gets a bit lonely being the sole proprietor of a business in the death industry, but when there's a story to be told, it makes sense to get it out.

Chapter Six

THE NEXT WEEK at my book club, the group rather hilariously picks Richard Matheson's *What Dreams May Come*, a story about a dead husband and his eternal love for his living wife. Luckily, we're the kind of book club that gets together at a bar instead of at the home of somebody named Gladys, so I'm heavily plied with gin martinis by the time we really get into it.

There's only six of us crammed into the vinyl booth in the dimly lit bar, but there's one woman who keeps talking and for the life of me I can't remember her name. Normally I'm quite good with names. It was Katie that encouraged me to join this book club when she saw how quickly I can get through a book, but I'm not sure this type of social interaction is really for me. While they are all crying about Richard dying and leaving his beloved Annie behind, (they know this is fictional, right?) I feel a numbness spreading through me like cold.

"Just the fact that even in the afterlife they couldn't *stand* to be apart," Katie sniffles before looking over at me briefly. "It's just so...so..."

"Perfect?" someone finishes for her.

"Perfect!" somebody else exclaims, "But she *died*."

"Sometimes that makes things easier," I say and everybody noticeably stiffens. Nobody can go up against the mortician commenting on death. I'm an expert after all. "People tend to stay the

most perfect versions of themselves once they're already gone."
People shift in their chairs. Legs cross, throats clear.

"Yeah, don't you hate how people speak so highly of somebody
after they're dead? Even if they were kind of sucky in real life?"
Katie mercifully attempts to steer the conversation away from
me. "I think that's because we've been taught to not speak ill of
the dead. Where did that expression come from anyway?" she
continues.

"It's actually attributed to one of the Seven Sages of Greece," I
say, hoping I'm being helpful. "I think it was a translation from something Diogenes, the Cynic philosopher, wrote. So that's interesting."
Nobody says anything after I've finished my little history lesson,
and I'm reminded again that maybe not everything that goes through
my head needs to come out.

"It's funny how sayings and traditions and customs are passed
on without us realizing it at all, isn't it?" one of the book club
people, who I think is named Masie, says.

"Sometimes those things give people comfort," Katie says.

"You must have thoughts on that, Mylène," Maybe Masie says.

I look around the room, gauging whether or not they're actually after the truth, or a more standard response.

"They can give people comfort, sure. But they can also hold
people back."

"How do you mean?"

I've been doing my job a while now. I can tell when people find
the funeral comforting, and when it's only an added stress, empty
actions in place of closure.

"Well they can be very sombre rituals, in some cases," I say. "But
they don't have to be that way. The whole wearing black thing has
got to go, in my opinion."

"Now that I think about it, I've *never* seen you wearing black,
ever," Maybe Masie says.

"I do try to bust through those clichés," I say. "Wearing black to represent mourning is a Western thing. In other parts of the world they wear yellow or purple."

"But some traditions are comforting to people. The familiarity of them. You're not saying that you think we should do away with *all* of our local customs, are you? Then you'd be out of a job," Maybe Masie says.

"I'm sure she's not suggesting that, are you, Mylène?" Katie asks.

"No, of course not. I'm just saying that you don't have to do anything if it doesn't feel right."

"But you have to do *something* when a person dies. You can't just do nothing. Every person deserves to be remembered."

I stare at Maybe Masie blankly. She seems to be one of those people who is either oblivious or impervious, but it's impossible to know which. Katie once again swoops in and redirects the conversation back to the book and a particular scene that she liked while I sit there and stare dumbly at my hands.

Maybe Masie has a point. You can't just pretend like a person's life had no meaning. I wouldn't be here today, or even own my business if it hadn't been for my mother. And maybe I should find a way to recognize it.

That night at home, I pull my mother's urn out of the closet where I'd stashed it, along with the small stack of postcards. I place the urn on my kitchen table and lean the postcards up against it.

"Do not stand at my grave and weep," I begin to recite the poem I've always loved by Mary Elizabeth Frye. It's my go-to when a family is struggling to find the right words to remember their dead, but this time the words just feel false coming out of my mouth. My emptiness thuds from within, so I cut the poem short.

"What would you want me to do with you, huh?" I say to my mother's ground-up bones.

As it stands, I've still only read the first postcard. It feels invasive to go further even though they're addressed to me. I pick up the stack and turn them over in my hand. It seems to me that most people would gobble up any crumbs left by their estranged, deceased mother, but I feel a sudden urge to burn them without reading.

The phone rings.

"Hello, Mylène Andrews? This is Randal Lahola, your mother's executor, calling again."

"Yes, what can I do for you?"

"I'm just calling to tell you that your mother's house sold."

"Oh, that's great news."

"It went for nearly $200,000 above asking price."

"I'm sorry how much?"

The only thing keeping the town afloat is the factory. Most people that live there work at it, and have done so and will do so for the rest of their days.

"The factory is acquiring properties in the area, you know," Lahola says. "They're actually looking to expand."

I guess you just never know what life will bring, what is bound to crumble or thrive.

"I just wanted to give you the news," he continues.

"Right, thank you."

"An associate will be in touch shortly to handle the transaction."

"Wait, are you saying…"

"Your inheritance, Mizzz Andrews." Lahola seems to purposefully draw the s sound into a z to highlight my singledom. "The money from the sale of the house will go directly to you."

It seems strange to me that my mother didn't have a friend or somebody that hadn't abandoned her to pass the money on to. I'm also surprised that she managed to hold onto the property for all these years.

"I know it's never easy losing a parent, but at least the funeral arrangements are taken care of now. That can often be a rather large sum, you know."

"I'm actually a funeral director, but yes, thank you."

"Oh, how interesting. Then you certainly do know."

"Right, well thank you for calling."

"Of course. Take care. And I'm sorry for your loss."

"Me too," is all I say, hanging up the phone and turning to face my mother's urn once again.

Chapter Seven

I PULL A wool sweater over my head and start walking in the late spring morning. I don't even realize where I'm going until I arrive at the gates of the Lakeview Cemetery. My body must have led me here, because it knows that people need to *do* something that will make them feel connected to their loved ones after they're gone. My body knows that you have to feel that closeness before you can start to let go. But the thing is, I let go when I was eighteen and never looked back. So my body is confused.

Though at thirty-three, single and friendless — or as I prefer, happily wedded to work — I guess it's not completely out of the realm of possibility that I do have a few things left to process.

The saddest funeral I've ever organized was one for a man named Henry Earnheart. He was the most organized person I've ever dealt with. About five years before his death he came to Gateway to say that he wanted to start organizing his funeral. He set up a payment plan and had the whole thing paid for in a matter of months. He said he didn't want to burden his children with any of the planning.

Eventually he died, obviously, and everything was set; the casket was chosen, the service was arranged, the flowers, the food, all of it. But nobody came. Not a single soul. The stack of programs sat there mocking his corpse throughout the entire service as his preplanned slideshow ran through his entire life. I have no idea why nobody bothered coming to his funeral. He seemed like a decent enough person. But there's a whole lifetime of things that can happen to cause people to be too busy to show up when you die.

I think that is a lot of peoples' worst fear. That they will die and nobody will care, that their life was completely obsolete and unimportant. But that won't be the case for me, right? Because I help people, I help families, and that means something, surely. Even if I do live alone and I don't have any real friends that have ever come over and seen the inside of my house. Maybe that's because it's attached to a funeral home. Not exactly everyone's cup of tea.

So anyway, I'm here at the Lakeview Cemetery. It's a sunny day and the fake plastic flowers sitting around the different graves look even more artificial against the clear sky. I take a small baggie containing some of my mother's ashes out of my pocket and reach in.

"I don't know who you were when you died. I'm not sure if I ever knew who you were, but I think it makes sense to leave some of you here, in a place I know you set foot and where you were thinking about me."

The ashes catch in the breeze and blow toward a different grave, where they come to rest on top of one Pauline J. Smithers: wife, mother, lover.

Lover? Interesting.

"Sorry, Pauline, these things don't always go as planned."

At least now I've done something. The rest of my mother's ashes can get stashed back in the closet, and I can carry on with my life.

It's my turn to pick our selection for book club this month. I tend to pick something really macabre and gloomy, as those are my comfort reads. But this time I decide to go for something more normal.

"So I've selected *One Day* by David Nicholls this time around."

"What an interesting choice! Not your usual is it? You must be heading off on a vacation or something."

The thought of vacation has never even occurred to me in my life. Small business owners just don't take them. But ideas are funny like that, aren't they? The way they suddenly drop into your psyche to fill up a space that was empty before.

"Actually, I am going on a vacation," I say.

Katie's eyebrows lift ever so slightly but she doesn't speak.

"I'm going to go on a road trip."

"You are! How FUN," Maybe Masie says. "Where are you going? Tell us, tell us."

It occurs to me before I say it that this plan I've hatched makes literally no sense. And yet, at the same time, that makes it all the more logical.

"Well, actually. I'm going to retrace a trip my mother went on just before she died."

"Oh my God, Mylène. You never told us about your mother. When did she…pass on?"

"Oh, she died a while back. I guess I just didn't really know what I wanted to do to, uh, honour her until now."

"Well a road trip sounds perfect. Doesn't it sound perfect, ladies?" she says, nodding around the group. They all bob their heads up and down in response. Their eyes are the softened, saddened kind of eyes I see so often on people that aren't used to being around death.

"It's really okay, everyone. I'm okay. It's more a, uh, celebration than anything. I just thought I could use some time off."

People always like it when you throw in the word 'celebration.' Most people are predictable when you bring up death; shock, recoil, regroup, excuse themselves quietly, and hope nobody asks any other questions.

"Well I think it's great, really. Good for you," Katie says, and I smile. Maybe she's right.

• • •

That night I sit down with a map and the postcards and make a plan. The urn is still sitting on my kitchen table, because it doesn't bother me to have her hanging around. I open up the package of postcards and start scattering them around the table. I start trying to put them in order. But then I remember that my eleventh grade geography teacher was more concerned with finding different places to get drunk at school than she was in teaching us geography. So I get out a map to help me with the rest.

"It looks like you went from Cleveland across northern New York and over to Boston...then doubled back through Southern New York," I say to the urn while tracing my finger across the route on the map. "Then you went south to Philadelphia, Savannah, somewhere called Key Biscayne in Florida, New Orleans, and finished it off in Tombstone, Arizona."

I have so many questions, what route did she take to get back home from the other side of the country? Did she sell her car? Catch a train? Hitch a ride with a trucker? In place of any definitive answers, the best I can do is take her back.

Chapter Eight

Granary Burying Ground
Boston, Massachusetts

Dear Mylène,

I've decided to keep touring around different cemeteries. It just seems like the right thing to do. I'm writing to you from a lovely little cemetery called the Granary Burying Ground in Boston. Are you surprised I'm here? And on my own no less. Well so am I!

In some sections, the headstones are the same size and shape, small and rounded at the top. If you stand in just the right space, they almost look like little teeth poking out of the ground. Have you heard of this place? It's where Paul Revere and John Hancock and a bunch of other white men are buried. And apparently there are over two thousand grave markers, but more than five thousand people buried here. I'm sure you would find that interesting. I like to think about whether or not you know these cemeteries and want to go to them or have been to them. I think you would like this one a lot.

When you were a little girl, you liked the old cemeteries the best. The ones where moss was growing on the headstones and the ground looked like it had shifted and changed. Because things do change as they grow old, Mylène. I hope you know that.

Yours,
Cerise

It's surprisingly easy to leave a place when you don't really have to let anybody know where you're going. All I have to do is forward my office calls to my cell phone, automate an out of office reply on my email, and make sure there isn't any cheese in the fridge that's about to go off.

And with that I head out. I gas up the hearse just outside the city and plug my first location into my GPS: Granary Burying Ground in Boston, Massachusetts. Did I mention already that I'll be driving a hearse? It's the only vehicle I have, so I don't have much of a choice. The plan is to sleep in the back. I know what you're thinking, that's morbid, disgusting! Okay, maybe it is, but don't worry, I'm not going to be sleeping in a coffin or anything. I packed a little air mattress and I even bought myself a little stove and a cooler. It'll be like camping. Although I've never done that before either.

Anyway, I'm on the road and this is going to be great! Well, not great, maybe, since I'm retracing my dead, estranged mother's route through a bunch of random cemeteries in a bunch of equally random cities I've never really had any desire to visit. And also, she skipped Salem? This is one thing I'm not sure I could ever forgive her for, so maybe there's just no point. But anyway, it'll all be something. Cathartic, maybe? Sure, let's go with that.

Once I'm out on the open road, it's hard to imagine why I've never had a desire to leave Ohio before. I graduated from Mortuary School when I was twenty, got my job with a Soul-Sucking-Corporate-Funeral-Home right away, and then opened my own business when I was twenty-three. And before that, well, you know the sad sack story. I don't need to go over it again. I'm pretty sure I missed out on a lot of life. On a lot of the regular, fun, coming-of-age, right-of-passage stuff anyway. I didn't even get drunk for the first time until I was *actually* twenty-one, at a corporate Christmas party. Oh my God, it was horrible. I ended up throwing up in an alley out back for two hours and everybody thought I was dead (ha ha).

So I've never travelled. I don't have any pets. I've never had a serious boyfriend, just a sporadic stream of curious onlookers who want to see if a mortician is as weird as they thought she'd be. I guess I've never had much of a life, because I'm pretty sure there's supposed to be more to it. But if you pay no attention to it, and tell yourself you don't care for long enough, eventually you don't. And then one day you wake up and you're thirty-three and you don't even have anyone that you would invite to your own funeral.

So maybe I can make some friends on this trip. But how do you even make friends as an adult, in a hearse, travelling around the country to visit cemeteries?

I drive for about six hours, until the drowsiness starts to make me nervous. I've always thought that I could never be the type of person to die in a car accident, caused by a driver who was asleep at the wheel, because I'm already asleep at the wheel of my own life, so it just seemed like it would be too cruel a fate. But given my state, I'm starting to doubt myself.

I pull in at a small diner that looks like it should definitely have The Monkees or the Bee Gees playing inside. I fit right in. Well my clothes do, anyway. There's a long white counter, with red vinyl stools bolted into the floor, and booths along the other side. The waitress is holding a pot of coffee in one hand, and trying not to look at me out of the corner of her eye, which is making the fact that she's looking at me from the corner of her eye all that much more obvious.

I decide to take a seat at the counter, because that seems like the best spot to be if I want to have an actual conversation with another living person. The waitress walks over to me and I smile, big and bright. It's my funeral director smile, turned up to two hundred.

You can't look too happy all the time when you're a funeral director. You have to look polished, professional, welcoming, and a little bit sad. I've got that part down.

"Hi there," I say. I'm really crushing this human interaction thing. "Do you —"

"I'm sorry, but did you just pull in here in a hearse?" the waitress says. She has one of those old timey name tags on, which reads 'Rose.'

"Yes, Rose." That's another funeral director tip by the way. Always use a person's name and use it a lot. It makes them feel seen and heard. "Yes, I did pull in here in a hearse, but it's not what you think. There's no body in the back, ha! Ha!"

Rose looks at me with her mouth slightly open. I can see her gum teetering there on her tongue. It looks like it's about to fall out of her mouth and land on the counter. I want to tell her to be careful, but I decide that would be a bad idea.

"So you just drive around in a hearse?"

Aren't waitresses supposed to be friendly? I'm asking rather sincerely here, because I usually eat all my meals at my desk alone, so I don't have much of a frame of reference. God, the more I admit to you the worse it sounds.

"I don't usually drive around much at all," I say. "But yeah I guess I do."

"Are you, like, obsessed with dead people or something?"

"I wouldn't say obsessed, Rose, no. But I am a mortician."

"A mortician?" Rose's pointy little chin juts out toward me when she says this, and it feels like it carries the same accusatory weight of an index finger.

"Um, yes I —"

"So that means you play with dead bodies for a living?"

"Well no, *Rose*." This time I say her name a little more sternly, like a disappointed parent. Or so I imagine. I clear my throat and try again. "Playing with a corpse would be illegal actually. A mortician prepares a body for viewing, if that's what the family wants. But I'm also a funeral director, because I own my own funeral home."

"Wow. What an…interesting…line of work."

"I think it is, but I understand it isn't everyone's cup of tea. Now speaking of tea! What kind do you have?"

Rose doesn't take her eyes off me, but gestures behind her at the selection of boxed tea on the shelf.

"An Earl Grey would be great, please."

"Of course." Rose busies herself making the tea and I run over what I can possibly say to make myself seem more normal to this woman. Nobody ever questions the funeral director when they're *in* the funeral home. Usually people are so consumed with grief that they don't think of the person handling their affairs as an actual person. But here we are. Hi, my name is Mylène Andrews and I am a real life living person, as it turns out.

"Would you like anything to eat?" Rose asks. "It's 2-for-1 fish tacos today."

I hope I cover up the look of utter disgust on my face quickly enough with my funeral director smile.

"No, I think just the…spaghetti sounds good."

"Coming right up," Rose says, which makes me smile even bigger because I didn't know waitresses actually say that.

The spaghetti is unassuming and tastes a little bit like the can it likely came out of. But it does the trick and I'm fed and watered and ready to go within half an hour. As I'm handing over the cash to Rose, I notice a rotating shelf behind her.

"Rose, are those postcards?" I ask as she hands me my change.

"They are," she says. "You want one?"

I had been expecting the postcards of local sites. Instead, I'm met with pictures of places near and far.

"You have postcards for Greece and Italy in there?"

"Sometimes people forget where they are, I guess."

"But we're literally an ocean away."

Rose shrugs. "Maybe they also don't know where they're going."

I can't help but smile at how absurdly right she is. I point at one of the postcards in the middle of the rack.

"Hand me that one," I say, not really caring which one she grabs.

The drive the rest of the way goes as you'd expect. Eventually the buildings make way for open fields and sky. I take the country roads and slow down my pace, and then skirt around Buffalo, before jumping back onto the I-90. The radio sometimes plays good songs and sometimes songs that make me want to drive the hearse into a tree. When I get there I only have an hour before twilight, my favourite time to visit a cemetery.

I love when a cemetery is located within a city, instead of on the edges. It makes me feel like somebody who was in charge of planning took a stance. Said that the dead shouldn't be cast away to the outer edges of existence, but worked into our everyday lives. But I tend to read too much into things. The gates look welcoming, and I walk through the rows until I find a comfortable spot. I also love that cemeteries almost always have gates. Depending on the family, sometimes I'll make the joke that it's the only gated community we'll ever afford. Sometimes it lands, sometimes it gets horrified looks, and I have to offer a discount on memorial jewellery.

Eventually, I find a spot that calls to me on the ground and I sit down on the freshly mown grass. I lean up against a tree and allow my spine to align with one of the spaces in its bark. The weather is slightly warmer today, but it strikes me that perhaps I should have waited for the weather to improve a little more before embarking on this journey. It would be much too ironic if I froze to death in the back of my hearse. These are the kinds of jokes and thoughts that get me in trouble. I should try to stop having them now.

I look up at the sky and open my bag, take out what I need.

~~Mom,~~ ~~Dear Cerise,~~ Cerise,

I'm here in the Granary Burying Grounds, just like you were before you die —

The tip of my pencil snaps off, because I'm pressing so hard into the paper. Not quite yet. I stuff everything back into my bag and get up to leave. Maybe next time. I'm not ready for any of this, I don't know what to say. It all feels false. Where do you start after fifteen years, when somebody is already dead? Do you know how much a person can change in that amount of time? They could be three different people entirely. Or they could have just stagnated and then died. Who's to say?

I head back toward my hearse and begin searching for a quiet place where I can park for the evening. Surely nobody will be brave enough to bother a person sleeping in the back of a vehicle for the dead.

Trip Log, First Leg

Route: Lake View Cemetery in Cleveland, Ohio > Granary Burial Ground in Boston, Massachusetts

Distance: 636 miles

Gas cost: $93.11

Spaghetti: $14.50

Bagel: $4.00

Coffee x 3: $8.00

Gum for coffee breath: $2.50

Total cost: $122.11

Notes: People, including waitresses, are not actually that friendly.

Both times I stopped to get gas, because holy shit it turns out fuel economy is not something a hearse is known for, the attendants looked utterly miserable. I can't possibly be that unhappy myself. I smile all the time, sure sometimes it's a bit forced, but I still smile. Those gas station attendants looked like they had never smiled a day in their life. And now *that* is sad. Actually come to think of it, maybe their lives are miserable and they are just making no effort to hide it. I'm not sure which is worse. But maybe I shouldn't be so judgey either way. Anyway, overall I think I'm glad I'm doing this.

Chapter Nine

Sleepy Hollow Cemetery
Sleepy Hollow, New York

Mylène,

When I was planning my route to all these different places, I knew, I just <u>knew</u> I couldn't miss this one. Sleepy Hollow Cemetery is in a town that's actually called Sleepy Hollow! I didn't even know this was a real place. How terribly ignorant of me. I'm sure you were aware. It is absolutely stunning here. I mean honestly, gorgeous. Huge, old oak trees and sloping, lush hillsides. It's like a fairy tale. Is that horribly insensitive of me to say? Maybe you wouldn't find it so. Forgive me if it is. This is the actual resting place of Washington Irving, the man who wrote the legend himself. And for contrast's sake, it's also where the timeless Elizabeth Arden has been laid to rest. Do you think she was buried in fine jewellery? And satin, or lace? How fascinating (and maybe a little morbid to think about).

I'm sure you would ask if I'm planning on going all the way into Manhattan now, to see the REAL New York. But the answer is no. I'm afraid of the traffic and the people and getting utterly lost. Sometimes, you just have to decide what is worth the effort, and what isn't. And plus, there is still so much ground to cover, and so little time.

Oh, Mylène, this place has certainly done something to me. I am elated to be here. I feel alive, truly. And I wish you were here to enjoy it with me.

Yours,

Cerise

Just before heading to Sleepy Hollow Cemetery, I stop at a little shop with a wooden sign that says 'bakery,' because it looks like the kind of place that will be home to shelves stuffed with both snacks and postcards. This time I have every intention of finishing one. The postcard, I mean.

A young boy wearing a green apron covered in flour clearly noticed my hearse when I pulled in. I know this, because he is looking me up and down as I walk up. Not in a creepy way. It's more in a way where he is trying to decide if I am carrying a stake and garland of garlic cloves under my coat. He looks to be about fourteen or fifteen, and I assume his parents must own the place, because why else would a child be in charge of the cash?

"Yes, I'm driving a hearse," I say before he has the chance to ask.

"Oh, I wasn't —" He stops dead (ha!) and I wonder what he was going to say.

"I'm on a bit of a pilgrimage actually. Very wholesome stuff."

He purses his lips and then tucks them back into his mouth. "What do you mean?"

"Well I'm…" I think twice this time. "I'm a funeral director, and I'm driving it to another location."

"There isn't a…"

"A decedent in there? No! Please!"

"Decedent? Do you mean, like a dead person?"

"Yes, just a different way of using the term, that's all."

"Oh, well…it'd be kinda cool if there were a decedent in there."

Are all people so hard to read? I mean, honestly.

"Right."

"Well, what can I get you then, Madame Funeral Director?"

I feel a kinship with him that I don't normally notice with strangers. Then again, I've not ever been in this kind of situation before.

I order my coffee and my Boston Cream doughnut, and I ask for one of the postcards that shows the Manhattan skyline, even though I'm nowhere close to it. Certain things are just about appearances, I guess.

Sleepy Hollow Cemetery is exactly as she described it; sloping and slanting and green and luscious. I find a place in the sun and lay down to read her postcard. I frown when I get to the end. It makes me feel annoyed, so I put it away and take out the one I picked up at the little bakery.

I've made it a point to only look at the locations on the postcard so that I know which city I'm driving to. Unfortunately cemeteries don't usually have their own marketing campaigns, so I force myself to only read the name of the cemetery before turning the card back over. Sometimes my brain picks up words like "gorgeous" or "fairy tale" and I make a game out of thinking about how that could possibly make sense. Luckily she's marked the names of the cemeteries on the very top. For some reason, it feels important that I never read what she wrote until I'm *in* the actual cemetery itself. Do you do things like this too? Set rules where they don't really need to be? It's not like I'm unaware that I do this. It's just I find a certain joy in setting parameters for myself and following through.

Or maybe I'm trying to make this feel more like the treasure hunt to understand a woman I will never know. But the downside of this process is that it means I have no idea how I'm going to feel when I read what she wrote. This one, I must say, is especially challenging. Particularly the line about knowing what is worth the effort and what isn't. See the problem with the written word, is that it can always be construed in any which way the reader wants. Was she suggesting here that I was not worth the effort? That she has no regrets in never once reaching out to me? That she is glad she didn't find me that day she went to Cleveland? Or, is she very annoyingly, very slyly, telling me that she understands my decision to leave her behind? More questions, no answers. I make a low snarling sound like a dog protecting a bone as I stuff the postcard back in my bag.

Though I must admit, I feel thankful that my mother only drove three hours before her next stop. My neck and back are already killing me from sitting in the car all day. Who on earth said road trips are a freeing and comforting thing? They seem definitively *un*comfortable at this point. Also, speaking of comfort, where was my mother staying during her trip? She certainly didn't have a hearse to sleep in outside the cemetery or in the parking lot of a Walgreens. Nor could I see her showering in community centres as I've been doing. Who knew I was so adventurous? Also, how long did she spend in each location? Had she quit her job? Was she paying for hotels? Do you think that she maybe had a *lover* in each place that she would shack up with for a couple of days? But how would she have come to know them? Oh, my sweet Jesus, do you think she was INTERNET dating by this point in her life?

Another annoying thing about her unsent postcards is that they don't have a date. I'm a pragmatic person, I like to stay organized. You may have noticed this already. But I have to be organized as a funeral director because I'm literally in charge of organizing a person's life. The end of it anyway. And so it *annoys* me to no end that my mother hasn't bothered to date any of her cards. I could guess, I suppose. But what would be the point in that? I have her death certificate and I could count backwards from there. Or I could pretend. But either way I would still be annoyed because it wouldn't be fact, just fiction.

So is this what travelling is then? Just doing very similar life tasks in different locations? Looking at similar stuff, eating similar things. Maybe it's different if you go to another country where they use wildly different spices? But here it's mostly just drinking bad coffee and eating stale sandwiches. Though I would be lying if

I said I wasn't enjoying seeing the different cemeteries so far, placing my feet in the same spot where she stood. At least trying to understand.

On the way back past the same bakery I make a last-minute decision to go in for a quick bite to eat. Everything is a gamble when you're on the road, it seems. So if a place looks like it isn't going to absolutely RUIN a Salisbury steak, you should probably give them a chance to make it for you.

The boy is still working behind the till, but he isn't wearing his green apron anymore.

"Hearse lady!"

"Yep, that's me."

"You're back! I thought you had to hit the road."

"Oh, well…I lied before." I've never been good at coming up with lies. The truth always seems to worm its way out of me.

"I see, I see," he says rather matter-of-factly, nodding his head, as if his weary teenage soul has already been lied to too many times to count.

"Do you want to know the truth?"

"Yeah!" he says. Sleepy Hollow must be quiet this time of year. Or quiet always.

"Grab us a couple of doughnuts and I'll tell you."

So I know what you're thinking again. I do, but I'm not hitting on this child. He just seems accepting, that's all.

"So what's the truth then? I'm Barry by the way," he says as he clatters a plate down in front of me.

I steady it with my hand and take a big bite, the jelly from the doughnut oozes out the side.

"I'm on kind of a…mission." I say this with a little lilt in my voice, wondering if he's already too old for folklore and mystery, but instead he leans in closer.

"What kind of a mission?"

"Well I'm trying to avenge someone."

"Someone who hurt you?"

"Yes, that's right," I say. I take another bite of the doughnut and nod at him.

Maybe this is what people do when they're on the road. Spin stories. Tell tales.

"What did they do to you?"

"I can't say, Barry."

"Fine, fine. I get it. So what's the plan?"

"Well you know Sleepy Hollow Cemete —"

"Oh, I KNEW it. I knew you had something to do with that place. My friends and I go there at night sometimes. We used to play hide and seek in there, but not anymore obviously, because that's kid stuff."

"Obviously." I feel a little bad, lying to him like this. I'm better at it than I thought. And I'm surprised he believes me so easily. Although the whole hearse thing probably gives me some clout.

"Listen if you need help, my friends and I —"

"No, there's no way. I'm sorry, it's too dangerous." I look around the room, as if I'm scanning for spies. "And you have to promise me you won't tell anyone about this, okay?"

"Sure, I promise. Scout's honour," he says, holding up his fingers in a salute. Maybe he is a scout, and he's used to hearing ghost stories around a campfire.

"Thank you."

"Wait, why are you telling me all this anyway?"

"Well, you seemed like you could handle the truth. Not everybody can." Before he can respond I stand up and tell him I have to go. I wish I had thought to wear a cape for this whole thing, so I could make a proper exit. "Goodbye, Barry."

As I walk out of the bakery I realize I'm smiling. Not my big, fake funeral director smile, but a genuine one. It hurts my face.

Cerise,

You'll never believe what I just did. I had just finished visiting the Sleepy Hollow Cemetery ~~(you're right it was gorgeous by the way. And I met this~~

I did what you wanted me to, I think. I went and I—
Ugh.

Trip Log, Second Leg

Location: Granary Burying Ground in Boston, Massachusetts > Sleepy Hollow Cemetery in Sleepy Hollow, New York

Free: 1 jelly doughnut

Drove: 193 miles

Gas cost: $30.00 (Note* is there a way to make this less expensive?)

Sandwich: 14.50

Spinach Soup: $4.00

Coffee x 2: $6.50

Dental Floss: $3.00 (Spinach stuck in teeth)

Total cost: $58.00

Note: People love stories as much as I do. Or people love being lied to I guess, but that's basically what a story is, isn't it? What's that thing that says that people who read books are basically just staring at a dead tree and hallucinating? Maybe that's the same thing we do when we talk to other people, minus the dead tree.

Chapter Ten

Laurel Hill Cemetery
Philadelphia, Pennsylvania

Mylène,

You must be wondering a few things by this point. Like whether I kept tabs on you all these years or not. I have to admit that I Googled you. Or, I Google you, I should say, fairly regularly. I've always been afraid that you would change your name and that I would lose track of you completely. But you never did, and I found that a small comfort. Like maybe you didn't want to erase me entirely from your life. Like maybe I wasn't all bad after all? That's how I know that you stayed in Cleveland. I read your bio when you worked at that other company. And I cried with joy when I saw that you started your own business. I was so proud of you, but I figured that would mean nothing, coming from me.

Anyway, on a lighter note, I'm here at Laurel Hill Cemetery and I've got to say it isn't my favourite so far. No offence to those that have chosen this as their final resting place, of course. Objectively, it's beautiful, well-manicured with sweeping views. And the elaborate mausoleums are always fun to admire, but a bit gaudy for my taste. I only stopped here because it's a historical site and I felt like I should. I guess that always puts a damper on things, when we do them only because we think we should, and not because we really want to.

Yours,
Cerise

I read the cryptic postcard with my back up against a tall structure that looks like the Washington Monument, but smaller. Like if the Washington Monument had a baby and planted it hundreds of miles away. The weather is warmer today as we inch our way closer to spring. The deciduous trees are budding now, making them look like they're blinking their little green eyes awake.

I frown at the postcard in my hand. My annoyance with my mother seems to be shifting into something a bit larger and uglier now. I'm getting pretty sick of her rhetorical questions, because I would have loved to answer just one of them for real at some point. What's the opposite of a rhetorical question? A question with a clear cut answer. I have a few of those.

Yes, I kept my name because I thought you would come find me eventually. Yes, I did want to erase you entirely from my life, but I didn't because I didn't know what was fair anymore. I didn't, and I still don't know who hurt who more and now it's too late.

You know what…

Cerise,

FUCK YOU!!!!!!!!!!!!!!!!

I scribble on the postcard until the black ink takes over the entire space. I press so deeply into it that my pen breaks and ink drips out of the end. The whole thing looks like a Rorschach test now, but I don't want to know what a psychiatrist would have to say about any of this. Though I do sense some sort of release. Did that make me feel better? Maybe a little.

I stare down at my attempt at a postcard in disbelief and then tear it in two, careful to keep the ink-covered surface away from my vintage capris. I toss it in the garbage on the way out the gates. Maybe I should consider doing the same with my mother's postcard too, scribble and draw all over it until the words are gone and I can pretend like they were never there in the first place. Maybe I should just do the same with all of them and turn around and go home.

Back on the highway, I'm daydreaming about the hot shower I plan to take when I get to my next location. The plan was to sleep outside a community centre again tonight, and take a quick shower in the morning before hitting the road bright and early. There's a lot of ground to cover between here and the next cemetery in Savannah. But just as my daydream is revving up, the hearse starts to shudder and shake. Thick, black smoke begins pouring outside of the hood of the car, creating a pillow-y stream in our wake.

"What the fu…" I say. "Is this actually happening?"

The hearse lurches forward once and then putters loudly and dies. "Really?" I guide it over to the shoulder and then get out to take a look, but a sudden rumbling sounds so ominous I'm worried the thing might explode. "Cars only blow up in the movies right? Shit! Shit."

Luckily my life experience has trained me to be prepared for anything, so I'm ready with my AAA card. It takes nearly three hours, but they eventually get me and the hearse to a local mechanic, who directs me to another cafe nearby where I can settle in to wait. Though I will say that the tow truck driver certainly gave me a look of a thousand daggers when I made him hitch up a hearse to his truck. Do people think that hearses are bad luck or something? Or is it that they think that it's cursed? Or do they just get the heebie jeebies because there was a corpse in there at some point? It's still a *Cadillac*! The audacity.

I order a latte at the cafe and sit down at a table in the corner and open my journal to sort out my trip log.

Trip Log, Third Leg: <u>HEARSE MAY BE DEAD</u>

Location: Sleepy Hollow Cemetery in Sleepy Hollow, New York > Laurel Hill Cemetery in Philadelphia, Pennsylvania

Drove: 134 miles

Gas cost: $20.00

Sandwich: $14.50 (rip off)

Soup: $5.00

Coffee x 3: $8.50

Cost to fix car: ???

Total cost: ???

Notes: Need to come up with a plan for if the hearse can't be fixed. Buy car? Go home? Take the bus? (Gross.) I suppose I could always —

Chapter Eleven

"I'm sorry." The man sitting next to me leans over and says, "Did you just write 'hearse may be dead' all in capital letters and then underline it?" He has salt and pepper hair with a well-trimmed beard and is staring right down at my notes. So his question is rhetorical too, and I've had just about enough of those.

"Excuse me?" I say. What is the eyeball equivalent of eavesdropping? "These are my *personal* documents."

"I know, I'm sorry. It's just, I'm a reporter...part of my job is to pick up on a good story when one sits down unassumingly beside me at a cafe."

"Well there's no story here."

"Forgive me, but it seems like there is."

"Sir, I —"

"Where are you from? This is all off the record. I'm just genuinely curious."

"I...uh..."

"I'm sorry if I'm being invasive. I've been in this industry for a long time. The lines get blurred sometimes. But I've found most people have a story to tell, if you let them know you want to listen."

If his eyes were any colour except that type of brown that makes you feel safe, I would have just got up and left.

"I suppose that's true. I'm from Cleveland. And yes, I was driving a hearse across the country, reading unsent postcards from my dead mother in the cemeteries she visited before she died. If you must know."

The man's mouth falls open and works itself up and down a few times before he responds.

"And you don't think this is an interesting story?"

"Well."

"Okay, you have to let me write something about you. Please. I work for *The Philadelphia Enquirer*. Here." He hands me a card. "What do you *do* for a living?"

"I'm a funeral director."

"Un…believable.

MORTICIAN RETRACES DECEASED MOTHER'S CROSS-COUNTRY TRIP

Philadelphia Enquirer
Philadelphia, Pennsylvania
By: Peter Fenton

It's not every day that you see a mortician jump out the back of a hearse while brushing her teeth, but that's exactly what I saw when I pulled up for our interview (albeit a little early).

Mylène Andrews didn't look or sound like what you'd imagine an undertaker might look or sound like. On the day of our interview, Andrews was dressed in a pair of cobalt blue pants and a white cotton shirt. Her auburn hair was swept up in vintage victory rolls and her piercing blue eyes were perfectly framed by her cat-eye glasses. She looked more like she belonged in a Broadway play than sleeping in the back of a hearse. Though, this reporter would also bet that the average reader doesn't think about morticians at all, unless they have to. Unless the unthinkable, but all too unavoidable has happened, and they are forced to organize a service for their dearly departed. But Andrews hopes to change that.

"I really believe in normalizing talking about death. Though I didn't actually set out to do that with this trip. It just seems to be a bi-product of it all when people see the hearse."

Having lost her father at a very young age, Andrews has always been intrigued by the concept of death, so she went on to study Mortuary Sciences at the University of Cleveland. When asked how her father's death affected her growing up, Andrew's eyes went a bit glassy as she looked off to the side.

"Well it changed everything. My mother and I kind of drifted apart after he died, and we eventually became estranged from one another. She just died a few weeks ago, which is what prompted this trip."

Andrews hopes that retracing her mother, Cerise Andrews', route across the country to visit famous cemeteries will help them connect, despite now living in different realms. Although it might seem like a post-mortem road trip would be a macabre or solemn journey, Andrews insists that she is feeling more lighthearted about it simply because she is so comfortable around death.

And while Andrews never intended to attract media coverage with her trip, her choice of vehicle certainly turns heads. Why wouldn't she just buy an RV, or stay in hotels you might ask? Well, she had an answer for that too.

"I don't like staying in hotels," Andrews said. "I never have. They freak me out. That duvet? You better believe that it hasn't been washed in ages. But my hearse gets scrubbed clean after each service. Plus it's the only vehicle I own and it's just comfortable. And that's what this trip was about, I guess, finding some comfort."

Mylène's business, Gateway Funeral Home, is currently closed while she completes her road trip, but she is eager to get to her final stop in Tombstone, Arizona, where she'll hopefully find some closure.

Chapter Twelve

THE NEXT DAY I find myself sitting at something called a vegan brunch at 1:00 in the afternoon with Peter and his husband Ralph. After I let Peter interview me in the little café, he asked how long I would be in town. When I told him that my hearse was broken down and I didn't know how long it would take to be fixed he insisted I stay with him. Imagine being so certain that a stranger isn't going to murder you in your sleep that you demand they sleep on your Egyptian cotton sheets.

Anyway, that's how I found myself sitting in this jam-packed hipster restaurant where Edison bulbs dangle from the ceiling (indoors) and drinks are served in quirky, mismatched mugs. And, *obviously* I've heard of brunch before, but I've never actually bothered to go out for it, and I definitely haven't paid good money for vegan food with all the flavour removed. I normally eat a set of standard meals *at home* because it's cheaper and the only person I have to try to avoid is myself.

"So this is brunch," I say, looking around at the people sipping different versions of pretentiously poured coffee. "I'm not sure it's for me."

"Pipe down," Ralph says.

"You haven't even tried it yet," Peter adds, with an exasperated sigh.

I can tell that we're already at the stage in our friendship where they find me both adorable and insufferable.

"You're going to love it." Ralph nods as he places a reassuring hand on my shoulder. The movement releases the scent of his aftershave, something spruce-needle-y. His skin is perfectly smooth, like he has a personalized ten-step moisturizing system. He's wearing the most expensive looking plaid shirt I've ever seen, but his raven-black hair is just the right length to look effortless.

"It's kind of like you're a Martian," Peter says, interrupting my gawking. "I can't believe you've never been out to brunch before. It's the best possible meal option. You want breakfast? You want lunch? Who can choose? Have them both."

"Plus mimosas," Ralph says taking a sip from the champagne flute in front of him. "Besides, with the vintage clothes and retro hairstyle you've got going on, you fit right in."

"How dare you tell me I belong at brunch!" The men laugh and I realize I've made a joke on purpose. Perhaps there is something to be said for having a willing audience. "So my first experience is going to be without eggs...or meat...or dairy?"

"I promise you, this place works miracles," Ralph says with a wink of one of his icy blue eyes. "This is the place that actually turned me into a vegan. I was a non-believer too when I first met Peter."

"And now look at you," Peter says, reaching out and giving Ralph's hand a gentle squeeze.

"You came over to the dark side and you never looked back."

"Ugh. You two almost make me believe in love." The mens' laugh crackles through the chattering crowd again.

"So I've got to tell you, Mylène," Peter says. "My editor *loved* the piece I wrote on you. She wants more."

"That's honestly shocking to hear," I say.

"Are you kidding? Your story is fascinating to people. *You* are fascinating to people."

"Surely there must be something better on TV," I say.

"Not since the Britney Spears tribute on *Glee* aired," Peter says, while Ralph closes his eyes and nods twice.

"What more could you possibly give your editor, story-wise?" I ask. "I feel like you already covered all the major plot points."

"Mylène, you're at the beginning of what is panning out to be a pretty epic journey. This could be huge, if you wanted it to be."

I shrug and take a sip of my coffee.

"You have to promise me one thing," Peter says. "When you get to the final stop let me interview you again."

"You mean this whole brunch wasn't on the record? Does that mean I have to pay?"

"If you give me that final story, I'll buy you anything you want."

I order an extravagant meal called Un-Chikun and Waffles with collard greens and a side of mac and cheese and spend the next twenty minutes telling Ralph and Peter how utterly revolting I'm sure it's going to be. When it arrives and I take my first bite, my soul instantly leaves my body. I had no idea that soy beans could be turned into something so closely resembling fried chicken. It's juicy and flavourful and it's deep fried, so yes. And who knew that waffles without eggs and milk can still be so light and fluffy? Apparently, you can whip the liquid from a can of chickpeas and add it to pretty much any baking and it acts just like egg whites. As it turns out, I would make a Faustian bargain just to lick up some of the batter. If having friends also means that they will take you to mouth-watering places to eat that you never would have tried on your own, then I've definitely been short-changing myself. I can't help but wonder what else I've been missing.

Chapter Thirteen

Bonaventure Cemetery
Savannah, Georgia

Mylène,

There are SO many cemeteries to choose from here in Savannah. This might be my favourite stop yet. It will be hard to top. This is another place I've wanted to visit ever since I read Midnight in the Garden of Good and Evil *by John Berendt. There's a statue on the cover of that book of a girl holding two little plates to feed the birds, and I saw it! I saw her. Why does it feel so incredible to see something in person that you've heard about or seen elsewhere? I have no idea. It just adds to the feeling of folklore and mystery and ghosts of this place. Do you love all these things too? If you do, maybe you got that from me? Maybe there is something I passed on to you that was worthwhile. Your father was never into this kind of stuff, he found it morbid and crass. Maybe it is, but I find it all helpful to think about.*

One of your favourite books growing up was The Witches *by Roald Dahl. You loved the part where they all took off their wigs and scratched their bald heads. Do you remember that? I do. I could see those witches having their meeting here at this cemetery. I hope you get to see it one day too.*

P.S. I learned a new word today from another person here at the cemetery: taphophile, a person who has a passion for cemeteries and gravesites. They told me they also like to call themselves Tombstone Tourists. That's me now. Is it you too?

Yours,
Cerise

It takes an extra week before I'm able to get on my way to Savannah. As it turns out some sort of rodent managed to build a nest in the engine of my hearse, which caught fire. Naturally. But it wasn't all bad being stuck there. I got to spend more time with Peter and Ralph.

Since I had some time to kill they took me to see the Liberty Bell, along with its impressive crack. You know the story of the Liberty Bell, I'm sure. But in case you forget your seventh grade history; it was ordered by the Pennsylvania Assembly back in 1751 to commemorate the Charter of Privileges. The bell came all the way over from a bell foundry in London, and when they went to test it, the thing *cracked* up the side. I love the concept of receiving a shiny new toy and then when you go to test it out, the thing splits down the middle like it has no interest in playing your games. Kind of perfect.

After all that touring around, I must admit that I was glad to have a comfortable bed to sleep in at Peter and Ralph's. I guess I am getting a bit tired of sleeping on an air mattress now. Thirty-three is not old, mind your tongue, but it isn't particularly young either. Maybe a bit more forethought on how I was going to complete this mission would have been better. But I do think that too much forethought keeps us from actually *doing* things sometimes. Like, the more you think about something, the more chance there is that you'll talk yourself out of it. And I didn't want to do that.

It's rather shocking how quickly you can start to feel at home in a place that is quite distinctly not your home. By day three in Philly, I was already calling it Philly. And somebody even stopped me and asked for directions, which I actually knew the answer to.

Saying goodbye to Peter and Ralph is much harder than I expected. The unfamiliar sensation of tears forming in my eyes makes my lips purse while I try to force the liquid back from whence it came.

"We're going to miss you, Madam Death," Peter says, already reaching toward me for a hug. Surprisingly, I don't even cringe or pretend that there's something that must be done in another room. Instead, my arms wrap their way around him and I pat him down like I'm a TSA agent. Hey, Rome wasn't built in a day.

"Say you'll keep in touch," Ralph says, wrapping his arms around the both of us so we're in a non-sexual three-way embrace.

"I...yes...will," is all I can manage as the rest of my feelings get in the way.

Once I'm back on the road it hits me that I'm actually going to be in Savannah soon. The place really does hold such intrigue and mystery for me. I remember seeing the cover of *Midnight in the Garden of Good and Evil* my mother used to love, long ago, and feeling really drawn to the place. When I flipped the book over and read the back of it, I couldn't believe it was a real place.

Now that I'm on my way, it feels unreal. An excitement is building in me that I don't think I've ever experienced. I wonder who I'll meet next, and if I'll feel at home with them too. I'm realizing it's a lot easier to meet people if you just start talking to them. (Who knew!) Working as a funeral director for so long has helped me get really good at talking about one thing and one thing only. You can't exactly make small talk when people are weeping, but I'm starting to see how much more there is to life than other people's sadness. Peter really showed me the value of asking some perfectly timed and nicely worded questions. It's incredible how quickly you can get to know somebody when you just open up a little bit about yourself, and then turn around and ask them to do the same.

I left Philly feeling like I was leaving two of my oldest friends behind. And you know what else? I know I'll be back! Who would have *guessed* that you could get in a car, on a weird mission and end up with connections that will last you a lifetime. Oh, and about the hearse, it's running fine again, after spending half a fortune to get the thing going. But I need it for my business, right? So I've got to get it back home somehow.

Philadelphia to Savannah is the biggest stretch I've driven by far, so I split it up and sleep on a dirt road off the I-95 somewhere in North Carolina. The farmlands have given way to meadows and rolling hills now, and I watch the sun set from the back of the open doors of the hearse. I still have more than 2,200 miles to cover before this is through. This country is too big for its own good.

Mercifully, I don't notice the rising temperature at night, as it turns out a hearse is quite good at keeping itself cool. But when I pull up to a rest stop a few hours further south it hits me when I step out of the car and take a deep breath. The air wraps itself around my face like a warm washcloth and I can feel the backs of my knees start to sweat. What a horrible place to sweat from. Do the people that live here just walk around with sweaty knee-backs all the time? No, they're probably used to it. Change is only shocking when it happens fast.

Soon after, I pull up in front of Bonaventure Cemetery. It's late afternoon now and the sun is filtering through the Spanish moss hanging from the oaks, making them look like they're on fire from within. Bright, fuchsia azaleas punctuate the grey stonework at every turn, wrapping themselves around the wings of angels, or the faces of cherubs. The marble statues point passersby in every direction. I suddenly feel like I'm Alice in Wonderland, and the Cheshire Cat is about to pop out and shrink me. No, wait. I don't think I have that quite right.

Bonaventure is postcard perfect. Near the base of one of the ornate statues, I take out my pen once again and begin…

Dear Cerise,

You were right. This place is unlike anything I've ever seen. It feels both man- (or woman-) made and like it could have just sprung up on its own. Though it feels ancient and mythical at the same time. Apparently they used to throw parties in here, and there's even a bench near the back where people used to come to drink martinis. Now that's what I call a resting place. And there's even a connection to Philadelphia here. A number of the statues came from a well-known sculptor in the city, but maybe you knew all this...

Trip Log, Fourth Leg:

Location: Laurel Hill Cemetery in Philadelphia, Pennsylvania > Bonaventure Cemetery in Savannah, Georgia

Drove: 727 miles

Car Repair: $1,200.00

Gas: $106.43

Food: $60.00 (chips, chips, chips, carrots, hummus, sandwich, some greasy diner food I'd sooner forget)

Total cost: $1366.43

Notes: Bonaventure is going to be hard to beat, if beating a cemetery is something that can be done. But I must say this is exhausting. Is it normal to be this exhausted? I'm doing less than I would normally do at work back in Cleveland. All I'm really doing is driving and eating and walking around cemeteries. Maybe emotional labour is tiring on a different level. Like a cosmic one. Maybe I'm feeling some of Cerise's exhaustion. As she must have felt that near the end too. I don't know. I don't have any answers.

Chapter Fourteen

I'VE HEARD THAT it's not good to text and drive if you want to remain alive, so I make a point of leaving my phone in the back seat while I'm on the road. Usually, that works like a charm. My phone ceases to exist and all I have to do is focus on finding the funniest radio hosts who play the least horrific music as I pass through each county.

But today, my phone refuses to be ignored. At first, I think it must be a wrong number, perhaps somebody looking for drugs or a cheating spouse, calling over and over in hopes of wearing their target down. I ignore the first few that come in, but when my phone starts to sound like it's going to vibrate right off the seat, I decide to break my rule and pull over. I'm hoping it's just Katie gushing with news about the latest book club pick, so when I unlock my phone, I'm shocked to see number after number that I don't recognize. There are twelve missed calls and over fifty new text messages. Thankfully I never set up voicemail on this phone, or I'd actually feel like I would have to get back to some of these people. The first text I open is from Peter:

I have been getting phone calls non-stop about you. I told you this was going to happen. They're all asking for your phone number by the way, but I'm refusing to give it to them. But I doubt that will stop them. Reporters are resourceful. Good luck.

The next stream of messages all start with some variation of: "So and so here, heard about your story. Would love to set up a call with you." None of them mention how they got my number, or what they *actually* want from me. Because there must be more to it than meets the eye. Be suspicious, children. That's what I always say. If Peter wasn't the kindest person I've ever met, I'd assume he sold me out.

Scrolling through the messages in disbelief, I wonder what it is that these people think I have to offer them exactly. I'm about to delete the whole lot when my phone rings again. This time I do recognize the number.

"Peter, what the actual fuck? My phone won't stop ringing."

"Do I really need to say it again? I told you so."

"Are you sure you didn't give anyone my number?"

"Bite your tongue. I protect my sources, even if they are swiftly becoming public figures."

"Great. What am I supposed to do? They're like vultures, circling my carcass."

"I appreciate the death metaphor, Mylène, very on brand. But you're the furthest thing from a rotting carcass there is."

"Fine, but how do I get them to stop calling?"

"Here's a thought…why don't you answer a couple."

"Answer them!"

"Why not? What have you got to lose?"

Radio transcript
Interview with: Mylène Andrews
Conducted by: DJ Bad Brad
CKGMY FM, 2011

Host: Welcome back, folks to CKGMY FM, this is your host Brrrrrrrad here. Today we have something a little different to talk about. It's a story that might tug at your heart strings and make you feel, eh, I dunno, a little weird. I am with, you may have heard of her, she goes by a lot of names…Mizzzzz Mylène the travelling mortician. Thanks for agreeing to come on the show, Mylène.

Mylène: Yeah, thanks, uh, thanks for having me on. Sorry, I'm a little nervous. I've never been on the radio before.

Brad: No problem at all. Don't be nervous, we're just happy to chat with you. So tell our listeners who you are and what you've been up to. In case they've been hiding under a rock for the last couple of weeks and they haven't seen the absolute media FIRE STORM you're starting.

Mylène: Well my name is Mylène Andrews, I'm from Cleveland, Ohio, where I run a funeral home. And I'm currently making my way across the country based on some postcards my mother wrote me…well, I'm retracing a route my mother took to visit cemeteries before she died.

Brad: But, I understand the postcards were never sent, is that right?

Mylène: That's right.

Brad: You discovered them when you went to sort out the sale of her house, is that also right?

Mylène: Yes.

Brad: Why do you think she never sent them?

Mylène: People do, and don't do, all kinds of things when they know they're going to die. They process their own grief and fear however they can.

Brad: So sorry for your loss there, of course. Very sorry. But you were actually totally estranged from your mother, isn't that right?

Mylène: I was, yes.

Brad: And you hadn't spoken to her in fifteen years, was it?

Mylène: That's right. Not since I left for college.

Brad: Right. Very sad. So what made you decide to come on this trip then? It's pretty wild if you think about it.

Mylène: Well grief is a very complex thing, it changes and it isn't linear. And when I got word that she died, and I found this stack of postcards in the back of her closet, I just felt like…I had to do something, or I would have stayed stuck in the denial stage forever.

Brad: You've been on the road for a couple of weeks now?

Mylène: A little over two weeks, yes.

Brad: And you have, like, a set of rules you follow?

Mylène: Wow, you've really managed to get all the details. Who have you been speaking to?

Brad: Ha, ha…oh, we have our sources. So some rules?

Mylène: Well, I guess the only one that I have is to just read the postcard from each place *in* the actual cemetery.

Brad: So, wait, you don't read the postcard until you've already driven to the place, found the cemetery, and what?

Mylène: Usually until I've found a peaceful spot to sit down.

Brad: I'm not sure all our listeners would agree with you that cemeteries are peaceful.

Mylène: Well, they should be. They're an eternal resting place, I can't think of anything more peaceful than that.

Brad: Alright, sure. Fair enough. And you stay *in* the cemeteries themselves, do you? Kinda creepy!

Mylène: No, no! Of course not! I'm sleeping in the back of my vehicle. Can I say that on the radio? I'm not even sure if it's allowed.

Brad: Sure, you can say that. So you're sleeping in the back of your vehicle, but it isn't just any vehicle, is it?

Mylène: No, it's a 1998 Cadillac Hearse.

Brad: She's sleeping in the back of the company hearse, folks! Can you believe it?

Mylène: It's the only vehicle I own.

Brad: I bet you're not getting the most incredible mileage with that, huh?

Mylène: Ha, ha. No, I'm not unfortunately.

Brad: So what would you say to people who think you're being disrespectful, you know, driving around in a hearse, not respecting the…mmm…*sanctity* of death.

Mylène: Oh, well I would say that I'm sorry that they feel that way. It's certainly not my intention to be disrespectful.

Brad: So why the hearse then? Why not rent say…a Prius or something? Hmm?

Mylène: It didn't even occur to me.

Brad: Alright, fair enough. So what do you hope to accomplish from your journey?

Mylène: I guess I hope to understand my mother a little better. It's not easy feeling like you've lost somebody when they're still alive. It's even harder to lose them without ever having the chance to resolve things.

Brad: Truly heartbreaking, Mylène. Truly. Listen, thanks for coming in. And listeners, we want to hear from you! Would you take a road trip across the country to visit the same places as your estranged parent? Join the conversation on CKGMYFM.commmmmmmm. Allllll-right, next up we have "The Edge of Glory" by Llllllady Gaga!

Chapter fifteen

Neptune Memorial Reef
Key Biscayne, Florida

Mylène,

This one is scary. I actually have to go scuba diving to get to it, which means I have to take a course, but that's something I've always wanted to do too, so sure, why not. Apparently this is a more eco-friendly option when it comes to burial, because the ashes are mixed in with some cement and it's poured into moulds, which are then placed underwater. Obviously I can't write to you while I'm there, so I'm doing it now, from the hotel. The Neptune Memorial Reef is technically a columbarium, by the way, (I'm learning so much on this trip) because it stores the ashes themselves.

I'm sure you've guessed by now that there's a reason I'm doing all of this. The reason we all do anything in life, really, because we know we're going to die one day and we want to make sure we've lived.

I've been thinking about my own death, and what I'll leave behind. I never knew there were so many options. I'd always just assumed that I would be buried in a cemetery. Well, that's not quite true. I never thought about it much at all. Does anyone? Now I'm seeing that there's a whole world of options out there, Mylène. And I don't know which one to choose. I know that I should just call and ask your advice, but that's one of the things that doesn't feel like an option at all.

Yours,
Cerise

The thought of being underwater really creeps me out. I have no interest in learning how to scuba dive. And to be quite honest I'm shocked my mother actually did it. Maybe she's braver than I gave her credit for. But I've come this far, so it would be cowardly to turn back. It means I'll be in Florida for at least a few days while I complete my certification course, but I suppose there are worse places to be. The air here is even more thick and wet, but I'm starting to get used to it. The palm trees swaying ever so slightly still stress me out, because how can something so tall and slim actually hold itself up? Maybe I will be safer underwater.

• • •

I'm struggling to balance my bag on my shoulder, as I have no idea what you need to wear to go scuba diving, so I just grabbed the whole thing. I'm also trying to balance my psyche, talking myself into actually showing up for my course later this afternoon. My phone rings again from inside my purse and I nearly drop everything on the sidewalk. The vibrating shudders against my ribcage while I rifle around in my bag, dreading another unfamiliar number appearing on the screen. I briefly wonder how much business I'm losing by being away like this, ignoring most of my calls, but something tells me it doesn't matter. The caller ID says Katie and I smile.

"Katie, hi!"

"Oh my God, Mylène. I just heard *another* story about you on the news!"

"Yeah, I know it's pretty strange, isn't it?"

"Well it's a pretty incredible thing you're doing. And you have an incredible story."

"People keep saying that."

"Well obviously it's true! Otherwise you wouldn't be getting all this media attention. You're famous!"

"I hope not. I don't think I've got the right personality for fame."

"Oh, stop. So where are you now? How is the trip going? I mean, I know how it's going, I just went and read everything I could find online, but how are you *doing?* Actually."

"I don't even know anymore. It feels like Cleveland is another lifetime away right now. So many unexpected things have happened. This is all going to take a while to figure out, what to make of it all."

"Well you are going to be one busy lady when you get back! I bet your business is going to go through the freaking ROOF."

I love that Katie says freaking.

"I'm not even sure if that's a good thing or not anymore. It's a tough business to be in."

"What do you mean?"

"Just that, I'm feeling uncertain I guess. About everything."

Katie gets quiet now. "Well that's to be expected I think. With everything you've been through."

"Yeah."

"Yeah."

"Well, listen I've got to run, but it was great chatting with you," Katie says. "Let me know when you get back to Cleveland, okay?"

"Okay."

"Hey, I was thinking, maybe we could read *Midnight in the Garden of Good and Evil* for our next book club, what do you think?"

I can't help but laugh.

"Sure, Katie. That sounds good."

"Great! I'll tell the girls. They'll be thrilled!"

Hi Cerise,

I promised myself I would get through this one. The thing is that this whole thing now feels bigger than me. I've somehow managed to get some media attention, and it seems like people are interested in what I have to say about death. I guess it's some sort of common, relatable experience that people want to try and understand. Who would have guessed! It's almost like it's something we all, LITERALLY all of us, have to go through. This is sounding pretty angry isn't it? Maybe I should try again —

Trip Log, Fifth Leg

Location: Bonaventure Cemetery in Savannah, Georgia > Neptune Memorial Reef in Key Biscayne, Florida

Drove: 501 miles

Gas cost: $75.00

Food: coffee, bagel, soup, salad, breadsticks, steak dinner

Cost: Forgot to keep track

Total: Unsure

Notes: Certainly weary now, and not sure I'm getting any closer to whatever it is I'm trying to find. ??? Right before I left Katie gave me a hug and said, "I hope you find whatever it is you're looking for," which I found strange for two reasons:

1. Because I didn't know that Katie and I were on hugging terms.

2. That I'm giving off the vibe that I'm looking for something? Or maybe she was just referring to closure. I guess people don't assume that their overworked, parentless, undertaker friend is entirely fulfilled, which makes sense. But I feel like I should at least have a better idea of what I'm searching for, because it seems like Katie does. So how do I figure that out?

TRAVELLING MORTICIAN'S HEARSE STOLEN, RENTS PRIUS TO FINISH TRIP

Paid partnership with Hertz Rent a Car

She's driven over 2,100 miles in a 1998 Cadillac Hearse, but that's as far as she'll get.

"When the hearse broke down back in Philly, I thought then that it might be worth switching it up. But I kept going, because I like to finish what I start. I guess I'm pretty stubborn."

But then things went from bad to worse. Shortly after getting the hearse back to the point of being roadworthy, Andrews drove it further down the coast to Florida. While Andrews was out learning to scuba dive so that she could visit the Neptune Memorial Reef on Tuesday, her hearse was stolen. Thankfully, all of Andrews' personal effects were safely stored in a locker at the dive centre.

"I've never been a victim of theft before, so it makes me feel kind of angry," Andrews said. "But it's one of those things you really can't control. So you might as well let it go as soon as possible. It's not good to hang on to that kind of anger."

When asked what the plan is now, Andrews didn't hesitate to respond. She isn't going to let a little thievery get in between her and her goal. "You've got to keep moving forward. What else is there?"

Luckily, Hertz Rent a Car has stepped in to ensure that all of Andrews' dreams can come true. Hertz has a way of helping Americans move forward. The company has graciously offered Andrews a free car rental for the rest of her journey. Although they didn't have anything in her regular style.

"No, we don't have a hearse in our fleet," a representative of the company said. "But we're happy to help Miss Andrews complete her road trip with a fuel-efficient Prius. Our most popular model!"

Andrews has two more stops to make on her tour, but she's keeping it hush hush about where they are exactly. Thankfully,

Andrews' options are open, as Hertz will also be waving the drop-off fee to any of their 2,000 rental locations across the country.

TRAVELLING MORTICIAN UNDERTAKES BATTLE WITH FUNERAL INDUSTRY

The Snowbird Post
Key Biscayne, Florida

"When's the last time you thought about your own mortality?" Mylène Andrews says as we take a stroll down Harbor Drive, just a short distance from where Andrews learned to scuba dive this week. While we walked, she took the time to inform me about some interesting death rituals around the world.

"In Indonesia, for instance, families actually allow the body of a family member to remain in the home, where they include it in daily rituals like praying. They believe this process helps ease the deceased into the next life, while also helping the remaining family adjust."

Although Andrews isn't necessarily suggesting that we adopt this type of ritual, considering it would be illegal, she does suggest changing up how we make decisions surrounding the idea of death, though her own view wasn't always so well adjusted.

After graduating from mortuary school, Andrews went on to work for one of the major corporations in the death industry, which she declined to name. If calling it an industry feels strange to you, it really shouldn't. Every year the death industry brings in upwards of fifteen billion dollars, and is slated to grow by over 40% by 2023. In Florida, funerals cost on average around $10,000.

"When I worked for that big corporation, I could see that there were some unethical things going on," Andrews said. "Funeral directors pressuring family members to buy things that were out of their price ranges, playing on a mourning family's emotions when they're already vulnerable and raw. And for a few years, I played along because I didn't know any better."

Eventually, Andrews realized that she was unwilling to be a part of a system that was taking advantage of its customers, and decided to go out on her own. Soon after, she opened Gateway Funeral Homes and has run a successful business for over a decade.

"I'm starting to think even what I've been doing isn't enough," Andrews said. "There is still so much more we should be doing as death care providers."

What she might do next remains unknown, but the whole country will surely wait with bated breath until she decides.

Chapter Sixteen

Lafayette Cemetery No. 1
New Orleans, Louisiana

Dear Mylène,

This cemetery might be a close second, after Bonaventure back in Georgia. I love that I can say stuff like that now, because I've actually been somewhere. Lafayette Cemetery No. 1 takes up an entire city block, and it has these things called oven crypts, but I don't think I have the courage to really learn what that means. Also, there have been a tonne of famous movies filmed here. Who would have guessed?

My final stop is going to be in Tombstone, Arizona, because that seems like a fitting place to finally make some decisions, there are so many details that need to be sorted out, that should be sorted out before you go. I don't have to tell you that though.

What I do know is that the cancer is spreading quickly now. I swear I can feel it crawling through my bones like a thick fog.

I keep writing these postcards, thinking that I'll drop them all in the mail at some point. That could be the first step. Better late than never, right? But every time I package them up and get them ready to go, it just doesn't seem fair to do it this way. You deserve an in-person meeting. You deserve so many things that you never got.

I'm afraid I'll go to my grave wondering who you are now, and what your life is like.

Regretfully Yours,
Cerise

I've got to admit that the Prius is a lot more comfortable to drive, plus the fact that it's free doesn't hurt. I would never have expected any of this: free car rentals, interviews, radio segments, perks! The man at the last gas station I stopped at recognized me as well, and offered to fill the car up with his own money, but I refused. There has to be a limit to this? I've now given over twenty interviews and read countless stories about myself, mostly accurate. One of them even said that I was on a mission to single-handedly change the way we think about death. Most of them claim that what I'm doing is either brave or courageous or truly unique. That's the funny thing about doing something 'big,' especially when you didn't mean to. You can take or leave all of the attention you're getting because you have no idea what to do with it in the first place. Or maybe it just makes you feel like you have no idea who you are anymore.

That night, I pull into a hotel, (also comped). It's easy to get over your fear of public sleeping spaces when you don't have to pay. I climb into the giant bed that night, with the plush duvet — that I requested be double bleached — and eat macadamia nuts from the mini bar until I feel sick. Then I settle in to scan the different channels, looking for myself on the news.

In one story, they've somehow managed to track down one of my mortuary school teachers, Patricia Bernstein. She refers to me as solemn and serious, but successful. Like those things are all mutually exclusive? I laugh as I turn off the TV and sleep a sound, dreamless sleep.

Downstairs at the continental breakfast the next morning, a young woman with brown hair and a Buddha tattooed across her left forearm sits down near me.

"Hi there," I say. (I'm an expert at this now.) "Are you travelling alone?"

"I am, I'm here for a women's festival in a few days. How about yourself?"

"Actually I'm travelling across the country to visit cemeteries —" I see her eyes drift toward the postcards on the table in front of me.

"No *way*. You're that travelling mortician, aren't you? Oh my god, can I get a selfie with you?"

It's the first time anyone has ever asked me this question in my life, and it's over before I have time to really enjoy it. This woman knows her angles.

"I think it's really cool what you're doing by the way. I'm sorry your car got stolen. But Hertz hooked you up with a Prius now, right? So much better for the environment."

"So true."

"I've actually heard that embalming is really bad for the environment too. Is that true?"

The glow of being recognized fades instantly and I can feel my eyebrows furrowing.

"Oh, I mean…it's not great. Er, there's definitely a lot of chemicals used in the process."

"So, is there a better way? Like what about that place you went to in Florida?"

"The memorial reef? Yes, it definitely is better for the environment."

"Because all the plastic and non-biodegradable materials in the coffin…they're really bad for the earth too, right?"

"I suppose that's true, I never —"

"It's cool regardless that you're getting people talking about death more. I, for one, like to think that the afterlife is just like one big festival in the sky."

"That's a fun thought."

"Well, I better be off!"

The woman and her peaceful tattoos bound out the door,

leaving me to my thoughts, which seem to be violently spiralling out of control. And I never even got her name.

That night in my hotel room I hide under the bleach-crisp duvet again and enter a deep, dark internet hole. I can't get the woman off my mind. Not in a sexy way. I wish it was in a sexy way. Her off-hand comment really rattled me and I've been researching the environmental aspects of death for the last six hours. It must be nearly three in the morning, but I'm too scared to look at the clock.

When I was in mortuary school, I remember one teacher mentioning the fact that embalming is a chemical process and therefore poses "some threats to groundwater through leeching." He also mentioned that cremation "can produce some concerning carbon emissions." But that was it! He glossed over it with the same, pretty death brush we use when we peddle polished mahogany caskets that are literally meant to rot in the ground.

My fingers seem to have a mind of their own as they enter different questions into Google:

"How bad for the environment is cremation?"

10,800,000 results. The first of which, you guessed it, is from a major corporation, spouting the standard line that overall, cremation doesn't account for *much* of greenhouse emissions. But if you scroll down a little further, you'll see that cremating one body creates the same carbon emissions as running a car through two full tanks of gas. And do you know how many people die every day? Almost one hundred and sixty-four *thousand*. That's two people every second, faster than the average person blinks. We blink every three or four seconds by the way. I know this because I've spent a lot of time in funeral homes counting peoples blinks per minute as a way to block out what was going on in front of me; the whole unfathomable grief thing. You get it. So this whole thing is an onslaught now. I can see why people live their lives without worrying about any of this stuff, because it's just plain easier not to care. Even still, something is shifting inside me. Is this what purpose feels like? Like a rabid animal foaming in the pit of your stomach? Who chooses this for themselves? But I can't seem to push it away. Thinking about bodies stacking up all over the world and needing to be disposed of in a way that doesn't screw the living over…well, it's overwhelming.

My fingers make their way out of my blanket fort and feel around for the dregs of the room service cookies that were dropped off at my door. I stuff another one into my mouth and open YouTube. Another hour passes as I watch video after video and attempt to appease the gnawing animal with more sweets.

It hits me that I stopped working in corporate funeral homes because I didn't like what I was seeing as far as ethical treatment of the families. I never, even once, thought about the ethical treatment of the earth. Something strikes me as so horribly *sad* that there was no course I took back in school called 'Environmental Aspects of Death.' Though you can bet I've now got a running list of schools that *do* seem to offer classes on the subject. What I'm going to do with that list, I have no idea. But it feels good to make lists. I've also written additional lists with the following titles:

–Issues with the Funeral Industry

–Ways that the Earth is Dying

–Most Fuel-efficient Vehicles

–Green Cemeteries in North America

–Reasons to Go Vegan

Families that come in after the death of a loved one are too distraught to really think about *any* of this stuff, and that's exactly how 'tradition' thrives. That's what makes things stay the same, because people just do things a certain way and *keep* doing them like that, because they never had some tattooed festival go-er sit down beside them at a continental breakfast and upend their world.

I have to admit to you, I feel slightly ashamed right now. The fact that these things have never made their way into my regular thought patterns is embarrassing. How have I never bothered to care about any of this? I guess it was easy to just keep my head in the dirt (six feet of it, if you'll indulge me). But how can we care about our individual legacies if the entire planet is already in crisis? I suppose I never felt like there was much to care about before. It turns out there is. There's still something to fight for. And if every industry in the world (looking you dead in the eyes oil and gas) made major changes at their individual levels, then we wouldn't have to wait for the government to stand up and make the changes themselves. Businesses have the ability to change the behaviours of their consumer. So why don't we? Why don't I?

God, the air is getting thin from up here on my high horse. What time is it? Where did all my cookies go? I need to sleep.

When I wake up the next morning, I shake off my sugar hangover and head for Lafayette Cemetery No. 1. Outside the humidity is around six thousand percent. It feels like you could drink the air with a straw (reusable of course, I'm not a monster anymore). But another thing has happened too. Not only is the heat of Louisiana draining me, but I also no longer care. About any of this. I spent ten minutes at the cemetery and didn't even take out the postcards before turning around to leave. I went to a café and ate three pieces of pie while watching the people walk by, wondering what it is that makes their individual lives worth living.

By 4:00 p.m. all I want to do is curl up in a place with a cross breeze and drift away. My mother's postcards have offered nothing in the way of resolution or closure. Instead, they've created an endless stream of questions. All she's done is go to some cemeteries to decide, what? What she wants done with her corpse? She could have called me for that, and nothing I do now will change the fact that she didn't.

Lying in my underwear in the AC of my hotel room later that night, I watch my ceiling fan attempt to move the air around the room. I feel envious of the fact that it has only one job to do, one purpose. And it doesn't seem to care that it's doing it poorly. I think about what you're supposed to do when you're feeling conflicted, what the people in the rom-coms Maybe Masie always makes us read for book club do. I pick up my phone to call Peter.

"Peter."

"Well hello, my intrepid mortician."

"I can't go on."

"That's rather dramatic. Why not?"

"Because there's no point. To any of it."

"You mean life? Alas, you've finally figured it out."

"Peter, please. I'm serious. I'm feeling —"

"That's just it," he interrupts. "You're *feeling* something."

"Try everything."

"Sure, it's quite a lot isn't it? Have you tried wine?"

"I feel like my whole life has been wasted," I say, ignoring him. "Or a mistake. Or something."

"Well, it can't *all* be a mistake can it? This whole journey brought us together. Ralph asks about you incessantly by the way, I fear he might be in love with you."

"I wish, I'd love to run away with Ralph."

"Well, I hope you'll be very happy together."

"Okay, but what am I supposed to do with my life from here? Just go back to Cleveland and pretend like none of this happened? I don't think I can."

"Right. Well, it's Cleveland."

• • •

They say that grief comes in waves, and that eventually the waves get further and further apart. But sometimes one will come out of nowhere and crash into you and pummel you and you have no way of knowing when that will happen. All you can do is take a deep breath and hold on. Wait for the water to settle again, and hopefully spit you back out, upright. But I'm not sure if that applies for people who are grieving the death of a parent and their life as they knew it.

Trip Log, Sixth Leg

Location: Neptune Memorial Reef in Key Biscayne, Florida > Lafayette Cemetery No. 1 in New Orleans, Louisianna

Car rental: Free

Scuba Dive Certification Course: Free

Distance: 872 miles

Hotel cost: Free

Gas cost: It's a hybrid!

Food: Coffee…

Total: Who cares

Notes: This is officially an all-expenses-paid trip now. How does a person even get into this situation? What am I giving these people in return for these items? Nothing is free.

MYLÈNE ANDREWS DISAPPEARS BEFORE FINAL STOP

Philadelphia Enquirer, Special Edition
Philadelphia, Pennsylvania
By: Peter Fenton

Last week, Mylène Andrews announced to the world that she planned on finishing her tour of America's graveyard at the fabled outlaw cemetery in Tombstone, Arizona. But since making the announcement there has been complete radio silence from the travelling mortician. She was last seen near the Louisiana-Texas border, though those claims were not verified.

Perhaps one of the most compelling parts of this sensational story, has been that nobody knew where Andrews was planning on going next, but when anyone caught sight of a hearse driving around their community, you could be sure they looked at the driver to see if it was her. More recently, Andrews was quoted, urging people to be respectful of the vehicles, and that she regretted leaving for this journey in a hearse, as it sent the wrong message to the general public.

About ten miles outside Beaumont, Texas there was a report that a bystander raced alongside a hearse, snapping pictures and distracting the driver. It was later found out that this hearse was actually transporting a coffin to a cemetery for interment. Reported sightings have been ringing phones off the hook in the Southern states, where Andrews seems to be focussing her tour. This despite the fact that Andrews is known to be driving a Prius now, provided free of charge by a rental company.

Interestingly, when the *Philadelphia Enquirer* originally broke the story about Andrew's hearse being stolen, Twitter was alight with claims of conspiracy theories. Some of the wilder ones insisted that Andrews drowned while visiting the Florida Memorial Reef, and that a cover-up has been taking place ever since. Of course, these claims are unsubstantiated as Mylène was confirmed to be in Louisiana shortly before disappearing.

At this time, police say that no missing person's reports will be filed, as there's been no indication of foul play. So if Andrews isn't actually missing, but has simply removed herself from the public eye, what has caused her sudden change of heart? Why would Andrews pack it in and skip the last stop on her mother's tour, thus leaving the original goal of her pilgrimage incomplete? The world is *dying* to know. Could it have been that the contents of the last postcard were just too much? It's been reported that certain media outlets have been offering to pay Andrews for the postcards themselves, and unless they're successful, we may never know.

Crews are reportedly parked outside of Gateway Funeral Home back in Cleveland, in hopes of getting an interview should she suddenly return. So far, the lights remain off and phone calls on the business line are going directly to voicemail.

Reporters have an expression for when a person comes along that makes a story truly come to life, it's called falling in love with a source. And Mylène is beyond easy to love, even if she doesn't believe that herself. She stayed with my partner Ralph and I while she was waiting for her hearse to be repaired, and in less than a week I came to love her deeply. It's concerning that she hasn't checked in recently, though something tells me we haven't seen the last of her.

Chapter Seventeen

OKAY, LIKE I'VE already mentioned, this story has a happy ending. Though it all sounds rather ominous right now, doesn't it? I'm sorry if it got a bit repetitive, or boring there in the middle. The thing is stories, *true* stories, ones that replicate life aren't really very neat and tidy. They don't rise to a natural *crescendo* and then unravel to the finish with a soft *denouement*. And this story doesn't do that either, because sometimes you set out to get one thing, and you get the complete opposite instead.

I decided on a whim that I was going to go on this trip. I thought it would help me understand my mother more. I thought it would make me feel like I could move forward, build a life, but all it did was make me (and the rest of the world, apparently) obsessed with looking back. Getting Stuck. Unable to process and let go.

Because here's the thing. The one major takeaway here is that there's a whole wide world out there, and that you have a story you need to live once you're *in* it. This trip made me realize how much I love travelling, and that life doesn't have to be lived entirely in one place. More importantly, we aren't solitary beings. We aren't meant to live alone.

I do have some people I think of as friends now. And don't worry, I popped a couple postcards in the mail, one for Peter and one for Katie. In Katie's, I apologized that I wouldn't be able to make it to our book club in-person anytime soon. But suggested that maybe we do it online in the future. In Peter's postcard, I thanked him for the original interest in my story. I told him I appreciated what he started. It's just that all the media attention got to be too much. I didn't even show you the literally *thousands* of other headlines like:

MYLÈNE ANDREWS REPORTED DEAD
MYLÈNE ANDREWS MURDERED?
MYLÈNE ANDREWS A CON ARTIST, MOTHER ALIVE

And it went on, and on. I mean, I know a lot of people were smart enough to see through the bullshit. But it seemed like the exact opposite of what I wanted was happening. People were not talking openly about death and dying and the legacy they wanted to leave behind. They were sensationalizing death, turning it into this obsession that it should never be. Because that's what we do isn't it? When somebody chooses to die by suicide, we ask how they did it? Like that's the detail that matters. We have such an obsession with how people died instead of caring about how they lived. What matters are our relationships, to other people, to ourselves, to the world we live in, to the space we occupy on this tiny rock hurtling through space.

I made a decision back in Louisiana that I wasn't going to publicize the exact details of the remaining postcards. Because the sanctity of some things truly should be respected. But what I will share with you is the twist I didn't see coming. You'll likely have assumed, as I did, that my mother knew she was dying and was trying to decide what she wanted done with her corpse. It turns out it was more complex than that. She was deciding *when* she wanted to die. My mother knew how limited her time was. She also knew that she didn't want to be a burden to anyone, that she didn't want to re-enter my life just as she was dying, and ask to be taken care of. Instead, she made the decision to die on her own terms, before the cancer could take her. She made all the arrangements, took care of every last detail, from the colour of the urn, to the prepaid shipping label to send her ashes back home.

She travelled to Canada, to the Kootenays near Nelson, British Columbia to fulfill her childhood dream of seeing the mountains. She said Canada was a country 'more underrated than our own,' and that taking the trip would make death feel like a final vacation. She checked herself into Sacred Temple Hospice Care, where medical assistance in dying was a respected option for end-of-life care. And after two weeks of hiking the trails during the day and eating chocolate cake for dinner every night, she chose to pass away in the late afternoon. In her final postcard, she told me that she was sorry, but that taking care of herself in death was the only way she could think to make up for the times she'd left me to fend for myself. She also told me not to worry about her being 'alone,' because she would be surrounded by dedicated end-of-life staff, the best the death industry had to offer, minus yours truly, of course.

So what happened after I gave up on my Tombstone Tour? Why did I decide to disappear? Well lucky you, you get to be one of the few to find out.

Epilogue

November 1, 2015
Dear Cerise,
I have too much to say so I'm writing you a final letter instead of a
postcard. I hope you don't mind. I also hope you'll forgive me for never
making it to the end of our little cemetery tour, though I guess it's kind
of perfect that way. So often things are left unsaid, or incomplete. Why
should this be any different?

You know, I've been telling people to keep talking to their deceased
loved ones for years, but this trip has been the first time I've finally been
able to take my own advice. I've tried to tell myself that I don't have any
regrets about not talking to you while you were still alive, because what's
the point of regrets? But now that I've gone on this life-altering trip, I
guess I understand the feeling more now. We feel regret so that we don't
inadvertently sabotage our lives anymore.

I guess what I regret is never apologizing to you for leaving. I don't
know what would have happened if I'd stayed in that town to take care of
you. Maybe we would have grown old together, or maybe we would have
grown angry and apart. There's no way of knowing now, and I have to
be okay with that. I try to tell myself that it was my leaving that made
you snap out of it. And that you didn't ever try to repair things because
you were ashamed, not because you didn't want to.

The good news is that I've invested the money from the sale of
Gateway Funeral Home along with the rest of the money you left me,

and bought property here in British Columbia. It's near Sacred Temple, because the poetry of that was too perfect to deny. And also there was a foreclosure so the land was cheap. Let's be serious. But I guess it did feel a little like divine intervention. So if you do have control of these sorts of things from wherever you are, could you do something about the land tax as well?

Anyway, I like that I'm close to where you made your final decision, where you took your last breaths. It's like being within proximity of your choice allows me to draw from your strength. Because it couldn't have been easy, to decide to die. So many of us walk around terrified of when the Grim Reaper is going to swoop down and take us. I can't help but be impressed by the fact that you stared Death in the face and challenged him to take you sooner. I want you to know I would have supported you. I do, support you.

I had your ashes pressed into a gemstone and set into the fireplace in the main building of our new community here: The Centre for Digni-fied Death. In fact, anyone that comes here to pass on has the option of having their ashes pressed into a gemstone and inlaid into the fireplace as well. We call it our mosaic of lives well lived. And before you jump down my throat about everything I've learned about cremation, we are now doing bio-cremation, which uses water and potassium chloride to reduce the body to its basic elements.

We have it all here, Cerise. I wish you could see it, and I'm not just saying that because it's a thing you say. I really do wish you could see what we've created over the last two years. Our bio-cremation facility is state of the art and one of very few operating in North America. We have a beautiful hospice care building, which was built entirely by volunteers from the area who believed in our cause. And we even used reclaimed materials in the interior. If you can believe it, we have an entirely vegan menu, sourced local, organic. Peter and Ralph are so proud. Right at the centre of the community is our green burial plot, where we can place people who still want their bodies returned to the Earth. Instead of being subjugated to the outskirts like I always hated, they grow into beautiful aspens and maple trees that give us a spectacular show every fall. But my favourite part of all is our death doula training centre. Do you know what a death doula is? We support the dying in the final moments of their life, help them cross over. I've loved making that switch. Because it's equally important to take care of the dying as it is to take care of those left behind. I have you to thank for that lesson.

I wish you were here,
Mylène

PHOTO BY TESS MARIE GARNEAU

Emma Côté is from a small town in Northern Ontario, where the winters were long but the books were aplenty. As a result, she went on to study journalism, English literature, creative writing, and most recently completed a postgraduate certificate in publishing. When Emma isn't re-reading or re-writing a novel, she can be found taking walks in the forest along with her dog Fable. *Unrest* is her debut novel.